OWNING UP

OWNING UP

New Fiction

GEORGE PELECANOS

MULHOLLAND BOOKS

LITTLE, BROWN AND COMPANY
New York Boston London

Copyright © 2024 by Spartan Productions, Inc.

Mulholland Books / Little, Brown and Company
Hachette Book Group
1290 Avenue of the Americas, New York, NY 10104
mulhollandbooks.com

First Edition: February 2024

Mulholland Books is an imprint of Little, Brown and Company, a division of Hachette Book Group, Inc. The Mulholland Books name and logo are trademarks of Hachette Book Group, Inc.

The publisher is not responsible for websites (or their content) that are not owned by the publisher.

The Hachette Speakers Bureau provides a wide range of authors for speaking events. To find out more, go to hachettespeakersbureau.com or email hachettespeakers@hbgusa.com.

Little, Brown and Company books may be purchased in bulk for business, educational, or promotional use. For information, please contact your local bookseller or the Hachette Book Group Special Markets Department at special.markets@hbgusa.com.

ISBN 9780316570473
LCCN 2023941624

Printing 1, 2023

LSC-C

Printed in the United States of America

For Alice Karangelen

CONTENTS

OWNING UP

So if the question is asked, What's it amount to? the answer comes sliding out easily: It's just a merry-go-round that stops every now and then for some to get off and others to get on, and no matter how much you pay for your ticket, no matter how many brass rings you snatch, it's only a matter of time before your place is taken by the next customer emerging from some womb to take the ride. So in the final analysis, it's merely the process of being taken for a ride, and despite all the bright colors and the hurdy-gurdy music, despite the gleeful yells as the amusement machine goes round and round, the windup is a hole in the ground where the night crawlers get awfully hungry when it rains.

—David Goodis, *The Wounded and the Slain*

THE AMUSEMENT MACHINE

THE FIRST TIME Ira Rubin met Jerrod Williams, both of them were in orange jumpsuits, sitting in the chapel of the D.C. Jail. They were waiting for the nonprofit guy to start the book club thing. Rubin was not much of a reader but he had signed up for the discussion to break up the monotony of his day.

Rubin had seen Williams on the cellblock and in the dining hall, noticed him initially because he was very tall. Williams was one of those guys who got along inside the walls due to his easy manner. At the same time, Williams didn't seem soft. It was how to do your time in here, if you could manage it.

As for Williams, he had first noticed Rubin because he was white. Weren't too many white guys incarcerated in the D.C. Jail. Not counting that period when those

January Sixers were locked up, and depending on when you looked around, there were times when there weren't any white guys in here at all. Not that there weren't whites committing crimes in the District. But unless they were carrying charges of violence attached to a gun, most of them walked until it was their time to go to court. It was an unspoken thing that some judges tended to keep whites out of the Central Detention Facility for their own safety.

So Williams wondered what Rubin had done to draw incarceration time while he was waiting on his trial. Why he had not bailed out and was in here at all. He didn't look to be a danger to anyone.

While Williams was pondering, Rubin started a conversation. He was seated next to Williams in the circle of chairs the do-gooders had set up, like, campfire-style. They could talk, because the "seminar" had yet to start.

Rubin leaned into Williams, nodded at the paperback in Williams's hand. "Did you read that?"

Williams nodded. "Sure. I've read every one in the series."

Rubin, who had the same book in his hand, shook his head with disdain. "I couldn't finish it."

"Oh, you're a literary critic now."

"The book was written on a fourth-grade level."

"The whole series is. But so what? Reading any kind of book is a positive thing. Not everything got to be Dostoyevsky."

"The characters don't talk the way people talk. And

most of the books in the series are about serial killers. If there were that many serial killers, we'd all be living behind walls with private security guarding our homes."

"It's fiction." Williams shrugged. "Serial killer novels sell."

"You telling me you like this?"

"*Like* got nothing to do with it. It's a way for me to pass the time."

"That Black detective?" said Rubin. "He isn't written like any Black man I've ever known."

" 'Cause you've known so many."

"Come on, man. *You* know what I mean."

"My name is Jerrod. Not 'man.' If you're gonna address me, do so correctly."

"Okay," said Rubin. What he meant was *Don't be so sensitive.*

The guy to the right of them, wearing a woven kufi with diamond trim, whose eyes had been closed during their conversation, said, "Y'all mind? I'm praying to my god."

"As-salaam-alaikum," said Williams, shifting easily.

The discussion leader, more of a moderator, who was on the young side, arrived. The men treated him respectfully but not with *too* much deference, as that would give the impression of weakness. They noticed that he had tried to dress up, but that his shoes were scuffed and probably couldn't get a shine, and that his ill-fitting sport jacket came off the rack from someplace like Kohl's. In a way this endeared him to them, because it meant that he did not earn much money, but still he had made the effort to dress up in their house as a gesture of respect.

He was introduced by Danielle (they called her Miss Danielle), the jailhouse librarian, who then exited to do some clerical work. That left the inmates, the moderator, and a couple of guards. All men.

During the discussion, the talk turned from plot mechanics to ruminations on the main detective character, and whether he was "real," which meant was he "Black enough."

The conversation went something like this:

"He doesn't seem Black to me."

"If they made the brother *too* Black, white folks wouldn't buy the books. So he got to love everybody, like 'Ebony and Ivory' or sumshit."

"He's like one of those people who claim they don't see color. Which means, you know, you must be blind for real."

"It's like nobody else notices he's Black or thinks nothing of it, either. Like, in the world of these books, racism doesn't exist. He don't seem to know it, either. Like when that Bush woman, *Condoleezza*, said that bullshit, that she never experienced racism in her life. He's like Condoleezza."

"My man's got a white girlfriend, too."

"Yeah, why is that? Why he couldn't have a Black woman in his bed?"

"For the reason I said. They trying to sell a whole rack of books."

"His lady *should* be Black."

"What, you don't like white women?"

"I'm attracted to Black women, is all."

"I am, too. But I make exceptions."

"So do I. Matter of fact, I'm color-blind when it comes to women."

"For real?"

"Only color I see is pink."

The men laughed. The moderator stifled a smile.

"You don't hear this kind of thing at Politics and Prose," said Rubin to Williams, speaking of the fancy bookstore in Upper Northwest.

"Sometimes you do," said Williams. "I been to some book discussions there, got lively." Williams looked him over. "What are you in for, by the way?"

"Paper hanging," said Rubin. "You?"

"Gun charge," said Williams. "But I'm about to be bounced."

"You got something waiting for you when you get out?"

"What, like a woman?"

"I'm asking, what kind of work do you do?"

Williams's posture straightened in his chair. "Trying to be an actor."

"I like old movies," offered Rubin.

"So?"

"I'm just making conversation, man. I mean *Jerrod*."

"Cute," said Williams.

"My name's Ira," said Rubin, and he extended his hand. Reluctantly, Jerrod Williams shook it.

After Rubin drew probation, he went back to stay with his girlfriend, Maria Lopez. They had reconciled. She had a two-bedroom apartment on Eastern Avenue, inside the District Line, just off Georgia, one of those brick complexes with motion lights hung on the exterior walls. It was Maria's place, which she had originally shared with a woman named Linda Rodriguez, who understandably didn't like Rubin, even though he contributed to the rent. Rubin tried to stay out of Linda's way, but she was never going to be into him, because Linda hadn't signed up for a second roommate.

Maria was Salvadoran, first-gen American. Rubin used to buy his daily morning coffee at the 7-Eleven on Kansas Avenue and Blair Road, where Maria worked behind the counter, a job that helped with her tuition at the Montgomery College Takoma Park campus. Rubin was attracted to her immediately and talked to her every day, as many men tried to do, and finally he wore her down. On their initial date he took her to dinner at Vicino, an Italian restaurant in downtown Silver Spring, which in its modestly charming way, complete with piped-in opera music, could be, on the right night, a romantic spot. At the time Rubin had been writing checks at two banks, covering them by going back and forth. He was successfully playing the float, and had cash in his pocket. It caught up to him eventually, but at the time of their first date he was good.

Rubin liked Maria's accent, it did it for him. He liked her work ethic and ambition. And he liked the way she looked, dark hair, big chocolate-brown eyes, a lush mouth, on the short side with real strong thighs and lady curves, kind of built like a running back. Didn't sound sexy when you said it like that, but boy, it was in the flesh.

Once Rubin got Maria in a dark room, he had her. For it was the one thing he was truly good at. He didn't just like women in bed, he *liked* them. When they spoke to him, he listened, he was interested, for real. He wanted to please them, he knew how, and he did. Rubin could go for hours if he wanted to, he could control it and he wasn't in any hurry to get to that intercourse thing, there was so much more to do first that was pleasurable and fun, for *both* of them. He did want to get a nut, shit, everyone wanted to finish, but there was no rush. Even the women who became exasperated with him and cut him loose eventually had good memories of Rubin that they carried after he was gone. Yeah, you could call him a loser (legitimately so; he was thirty-two years old, after all, had been in jail, and didn't seem to be "progressing"), but he did one thing right. For women, Ira Rubin was hard to forget.

Now he was back with Maria (and Linda, who called him "the convict") in her spot. Maria had gotten Rubin a job on her cousin Julito's landscaping crew, as he had to have a job as a condition of his probation. Julito was an easygoing guy, he had looked Rubin over and hired him, even though he assumed (correctly) that Rubin would never work as hard as the Latino guys on his crew. To

Rubin it was just another job in a succession of them, but for the Latinos it was a vehicle to get somewhere, plus they seemed to take pride in a hard day's work. They were highly motivated and he was Ira Rubin.

Julito put him on grass-and-leaf-blower duty, the least physical task. Rubin came up behind the sweaty guys who were mowing the lawns (with those wide-ass mowers, they could do a yard in five minutes) and cleaned up the driveways and porches. He wore the blower unit on his back.

Rubin figured he was one of the only, if not *the* only, Jewish guys on a landscaping crew in the D.C. area. The Spanish guys on the crew (he knew it wasn't currently correct but Rubin still used the term *Spanish* in his head) were not unkind to him, and if they were not particularly friendly they looked upon him with amusement and a little bit of curiosity (they knew he'd recently come out of jail so there was some man-respect attached to that). Rubin had enough self-awareness to see these guys with some degree of awe—and also some degree of bewilderment at his own place in life. His people had been here for over a hundred years and he was nowhere. These guys had been in America a few years, spoke little or heavily accented English, and were already buying and building houses for themselves and their families. Sometimes, briefly, he'd think, *Maybe there's something wrong with me.*

He only had to look at his own family and relatives to see that. Jewish people in America were generally successful and smart. Sure, it was a stereotype, albeit a positive one, but it was fairly accurate. Some of his relatives were white-collar professionals, some had liquor stores and independent grocery stores (that wisely sold beer and wine), but whatever they wore to work, tie or open-necked shirt, all of them owned real estate and had made money. Not Rubin.

At family get-togethers Ira was tolerated and, one could say, loved, but not really respected. He had grown up in Chevy Chase D.C., his father in real estate, his mother a lawyer representing nonprofits. Now he was living east of Georgia Avenue in a building with crime lights. He brought his Latina girlfriend along to Passover. They liked her, and were not surprised when they met her, because Rubin had a type. At this point, no one expected much of Rubin, they had pretty much accepted his place in life. His brother, David, worked in finance and ran the Wells Fargo office in Baltimore. Rubin blew leaves off driveways and was on probation. His father said, "At least you didn't draw time." Hardly an accomplishment.

But Rubin didn't think too hard on his situation. He was an optimist. It would turn around for him someday. When he wrote bad checks, he thought, *I'll cover them*. In the eyes of the law, what he did was a crime, but to him it was one that was victimless. His uncle Irving, Rubin's role model, told him early on that passing the occasional bad check hurt no one. "Everything's insured," said Irving. "So there should be no guilt." In his own mind, Rubin wasn't a criminal, because criminals hurt people. He was just trying to get along.

He was out at dinner with Maria one night, they had gone to a film at the AFI Theater in Silver Spring, an old Robert Siodmak picture called *Cry of the City* (while it wasn't her thing, she tolerated his interest in repertory film), and now they were eating enchiladas and pupusas at a place on Fenton Street. The Latino waiter had initially spoken to Rubin in Spanish. It wasn't just that he was with Maria. Rubin was on the dark-skinned side, with dark hair and eyes. Some of the Black kids at Wilson, his public high school, had nicknamed him "Rubin the Cuban." "I'm a Sephardic Jew," he'd say to them, but that didn't disabuse them of overusing the moniker.

"What'd you think of the movie?" said Rubin.

"It was okay," said Maria without enthusiasm. "Who was that main guy?"

"Victor Mature. Handsome sonofabitch, right? A very natural actor, too."

"Yeah, I like him. Even the bad guy, I like him, too."

"Richard Conte. He wasn't *all* bad. He couldn't help himself, like. Product of his environment and all that. Conte was dependable. He was the lead in this picture I really liked, *Thieves' Highway.*"

"Is that one black-and-white, too?"

"Why?"

"Maybe we could see a movie in color some time, Ira."

"Next time, you pick the movie. I promise."

"Thank you."

The waiter had cleared their plates. They were finishing a carafe of red.

"I saw this thing on the internet today," said Rubin. "Like, a casting call."

"What does that mean?"

"Like when someone casts actors in a part."

"You gonna be an actor now?" Her tone told him she was doubtful he'd do it, or follow through, like it was another short-lived scheme of his.

"No, not me, not a real actor. This was for extras, what they call background. The people who are standing around or moving in the shot. Like in that movie we saw tonight, all of the street scenes in New York, where you saw people walking on the sidewalk past the main actors, while they were doing their lines?"

"That's a job?"

"Yeah. I mean, I saw the casting call and I thought it would be a kick. It pays money…Look, this landscaping thing is seasonal, and Julito is about to shut it down for the winter. I'll still work for him while he's up."

"Don't screw him, Ira."

"I won't." Rubin put his hand over hers. "I appreciate you hooking me up with him. I'm not going to let Julito down, or you."

"Okay."

"I'm just going to check this out. I don't even know if they'll hire me. I don't know how it works. But I want to make some money. For us. Maybe we can, you know, get our own place. I don't think Linda likes me."

"She doesn't. But slow down, Ira. I'm okay the way I am."

"I'll say." He smiled. "You're a beauty."

"You're so nice to me."

"I like you, Maria." He rolled the "r" when he said her name. It was the best he could do. He wished like hell he knew more Spanish, but like a dumbass he'd taken French in high school instead. And he never did learn a lick of French.

"I like you, too."

"So," said Rubin, "could you use my phone to take a photo of me in the apartment when we go back? I need what they call a headshot."

"Sure."

"And then we could take some other photos."

"If you'd like."

"I mean, we could do a lot of things. We have time."

"You're planning a long night."

"Con tu permiso."

"That's very good."

"There's an app on my phone, English to Spanish. I cheated."

"But you took the initiative," she said. "I'm impressed."

"I'm trying," said Rubin. He *was* trying, for now.

———

Rubin emailed his headshot (him in front of a white wall in the apartment, taken by Maria) and his basic physical description (5'10", 175 pounds) to the background-casting agency, per the instructions on their website. This was not a place where you went to audition for a speaking part, but rather a kind of clearinghouse for background players. He got a call a few days later telling him that he had been chosen as an extra for a production shooting in Baltimore.

After some give-and-take discussion, Maria agreed to let him borrow her car, a high-mileage Kia sedan. After all, he reasoned, she had only to walk across the enclosed pedestrian bridge over the Metro tracks, from their apartment on Eastern Avenue, to get to her classes at Montgomery College.

"How will I get to my job?" said Maria. She was speaking of the 7-Eleven on Kansas Avenue, which was roughly two miles away.

"I'll give you Uber money, and then some," said Rubin.

No one liked to lose the use of their wheels, Rubin knew that. He mentally made a note to make it up to her, to do something extra nice. Date night, to a movie shot in color in this current century? Yes, but something nicer than that, too.

He drove up to Baltimore, to the production offices in a large building in what looked to be a warehouse district on Ponca Street, south of Lombard, off 895. There he got a Covid test from a woman in blue scrubs, then was fitted for three different outfits in the costume area, located in the entire top floor of the offices. The show was set in the early '70s, he had been told as much. He had no life experience from that era, so he couldn't know if the clothes he would be wearing accurately represented the clothing from that decade. But the people who were fitting him seemed professional enough, efficient if not particularly interested in him personally.

The environment was controlled; there were people watching, non-uniformed security, to ensure that he didn't wander off into places where he didn't belong.

Shortly thereafter, he was notified of his call time and location for the following day. He reported for work in the morning. That's when he ran into Jerrod Williams.

———————

They were in "holding," a large space where the background waited for their scenes after they had been costumed. Today the holding area was in the basement of a church in West Baltimore, the location for the day's exteriors. There were rows of hair and makeup people working on extras, wigging them and fixing their period hair, in front of travel stations, large mirrors framed by globular light bulbs. Rubin had seen Williams seated by himself, came up on him and greeted him jovially. Williams seemed surprised but not overjoyed, or joyed at all.

"My *man*," said Rubin.

"Aw, shit."

"Never thought I'd see you again. And here we are, in Baltimore."

Rubin had a seat in a folding chair close to Williams.

"Did I ask you to sit?" said Williams.

"You're not having a conversation with anyone else."

"That's by choice."

"How long you been out?" said Rubin.

"Keep your voice down. Don't everybody need to know my business."

"How long?" said Rubin.

"I *been* out."

"Talk about it."

"You read about those police officers in the Seventh District, got in trouble for confiscating guns but not arresting some of the people they took the guns off of? One of those crime-suppression teams they got. Anyway, they were turning the guns in to evidence control but not making arrests."

"Yeah, I read about it, but so what? They took a gun off of you *and* arrested you, Jerrod."

"Wasn't my gun. But you don't need to concern yourself with that. I'm saying, because it was one of the same police officers in that unit who locked me up, my lawyer got the court to throw out my charges."

"Congratulations."

A silence fell between them. Rubin waited, waited…

"Aren't you gonna ask about me?"

"Wasn't going to, no."

"My court date came up, and what do you know, I drew a judge named Rosenbloom. He took one look at my name and his eyes softened. Judge Rosenbloom wasn't

about to put a man named Ira Rubin into the prison system. Not for a little old nonviolent offense like passing
bad paper."

"On account of you're Jewish. He said that?"

"Of course not. Anyway, I drew probation. Two years,
because it wasn't my first offense. The condition is, I gotta
have a job. I already *have* a job, but it's seasonal."

"What you doing, mowing lawns or sumshit?"

"My work is weather-dependent, yeah. Hence, I'm
moving on to this. Thought I'd check it out."

Williams looked at Rubin out of the corner of his eye.

"Why are *you* here?" said Rubin.

"Think I told you once before, I'm trying to be an
actor."

"This isn't acting. I mean, background extras don't
have lines or anything, do they?"

"Working on it," said Williams.

They watched the other extras in the room. There
were many, dressed, made-up, and ready to go. Crew on
headsets walking around. It was fascinating to Rubin. All
of these people, a part of something, *making* something
together.

A youngish guy came into the room, a light-skinned
Black man with dreads, had a clipboard, had all kinds
of things clothes-pinned to his jacket and shirt, wore a
headset, had a walkie in a holster. To Rubin he looked
important.

"That's a producer?" said Rubin.

"Nah, producers don't have all that gear on them and

they don't work that hard. This dude is the Second-Second AD. Him and the First AD run the set. See that clipboard? That's what they call the skins. It's a list of us extras, identified by numbers…You're supposed to have a check-in number. You got one, right?"

"Twenty-six."

"He's about to break the background. If he calls your number, you're working the next scene."

The Second-Second, a Rastafarian who went by "Ras" Mike, called Rubin's number. Williams got called up, too.

———————

They stood now on a Baltimore street, one of those wide blocks on the eastern edge of Highlandtown, above Canton, east of Patterson Park. The row homes had stoops and some were fronted in Formstone, a typical Baltimore setup. Period cars, what were called picture cars, had replaced the late-model cars that had been parked along the curb. The people who owned the cars were in costumes, too. Some of them were reading or sleeping behind the wheels of the cars. And then there were the actors and extras in their period costumes. Put together, it looked like Baltimore in 1972.

Rubin and Williams were among a group of extras, Black and white, who were playing folks standing in front of a house whose realtor had refused to sell to a Black buyer. They were protesters, aligned together for a cause. Some of them had been given handheld signs reflecting their views.

"That's what this movie is about?" said Rubin to Williams, after Ras Mike had explained the scene to the group.

"Pretty much," said Williams. "There's this white woman, see, she lives in Roland Park, the nice part of town, and she's had this Black housekeeper for many years, a woman she's become friendly with. Gives her a nice bonus at Christmastime, asks after her children, like that. The script calls the Black woman a housekeeper, because they're too correct to call her a maid. Anyway, the maid has a son, she's worked hard, fingers-to-the-bone shit, to help put him through college and all that, and now he's a young professional, and he and his wife are trying to buy this house. But the realtor has done some sneaky shit so that he doesn't have to sell it to him, 'cause he's trying to sell some other houses on the street, and he, the realtor that is, doesn't want the values to get driven down on account of a brother moved into the neighborhood."

"So, the opposite of blockbusting."

"You know about that?"

"Sure."

"You're not as stupid as you look."

"Thanks. So, let me guess: The white woman likes her Black maid, the white woman's not racist or anything close to it, but she's never really thought about the maid's life, her day-to-day or her inner life. But now she's getting involved in this anti-segregation thing here and she's becoming enlightened. Am I right?"

"That's the white woman's arc. That's correct."

"So the movie is really about her."

"It's about her *journey*."

"I've seen this one before."

"Me too," said Williams. "The people at the network are slick. They can do this social-relevant stuff and be on the right side of the angels. They like to keep it Black... but not *too* Black. And in the end, when the son gets his house, and all these Black and white folks holding hands and singing campfire songs and shit, the white part of the audience gets to feel real good about themselves. Like, all this happened long ago, we did our part to make it right, and there isn't any racism anymore."

"That's true, though, isn't it?" Rubin looked sincerely into Williams's eyes. "That means you and I can be friends. *Real* friends. Because we're all the same, deep down inside."

"*Fuck* you, man," said Williams.

As the crew set up for the first shot, Ras Mike came up on the group of background and addressed them. He told them that, at the beginning of the scene, they should all chant, "No segregation, no racism!" but as soon as he gave them the cutthroat sign, off camera, the extras should stop actually saying those words and mouth them silently instead. This was so the Sound Department could best record the dialogue from the lead actress, supporting actress, and day players.

"You all should be angry," said Ras Mike. "But not violently angry. It's a peaceful protest."

"So, tamped-down anger," said Williams to Ras Mike.

"Something like that," said Ras Mike, tiredly. He was a busy guy who was not looking to further complicate his day.

"Why am I here, Mike?" said Williams. "I'm just trying to figure out my character."

"Your motivation? It's one-hundred-and-fifty-eight dollars a day plus a free meal. Anything else, Jerrod?"

"No, I'm good."

After Ras Mike had walked away, Rubin said, "Why you trying to antagonize that guy?"

"He knows I'm kidding," said Williams. "We've had this kind of conversation before. And you heard him say my name. He remembers me. That's all I'm trying to do, make my mark. I got ambition."

Williams might have said, "Unlike you," but he held his tongue. Rubin was a loser, but there was no reason to be cruel about it. He wasn't a bad guy.

At lunch, in the basement of a different church, Rubin and Williams ate together at a table among the other extras. Background got their lunch, buffet-style, from a different set of food tables than the crew and talent, and the Teamsters, who ate first, per their contract. But the actual offerings were the same, and the spread was bountiful.

"This is *cash* good," said Rubin, using a D.C. expression that Williams hadn't heard in a while. Rubin's plate was stacked, along with his salad bowl, two glasses of lemonade, and a dessert.

"The crew eats like kings every day," said Williams. "And don't you know, I hear them complain about the food."

"Same catering service, I guess it all starts to taste the same after a week or so. But it's six o'clock at night. Why do they call it lunch?"

"It's *always* called lunch. Could be two a.m., whenever you have first meal, it's *still* called lunch."

"We working late tonight?"

"We got to finish the scene we started before we lose the light, and then we're wrapped. We sort of got featured in that protest scene, so they can't repeat us for anything else."

"For the whole shoot?"

"No, I'm working again. Courtroom scene coming up, I'm in the gallery. It's cool if I'm sitting down. But that will probably be it for me. *You'll* get asked back, maybe. I stand out too much, on account of my height. They burned me on that scene today. My size works against me."

"How'd you get up here?" said Rubin.

"Took a train, then an Uber from the station."

"That's most of your day's salary."

"I'm serious about this."

"I'll drive you home tonight. And then, if I'm working tomorrow, too, we can drive up together."

"Surprised you got wheels."

"It's my girlfriend's car."

"I don't know…"

"Relax. It's not like I'm trying to be your pen pal or sumshit."

"Don't say *pen pal* to a dude who's been locked up."

"Point taken," said Rubin.

"I appreciate the ride."

————————

Rubin turned in his costume after he was wrapped. He tried to flirt a little with the Spanish girl who was taking his wardrobe and putting it on hangers marked with size notations. Rubin thought of himself as somewhat of an expert on the origins of the Brown women he fancied.

"Dominican, right?" said Rubin to the young woman, whose skin was rather dark. "I been to the DR once. Loved it."

"Wrong," said the woman.

"Puerto Rican?" said Rubin, his second guess.

"You're done for the day," said the woman. "Bye."

Rubin gave a backward thumb-jerk to Williams, who was turning in his own costume. It was a signal that he would meet him outside. Then Rubin walked out of the costume department, unfazed by the rejection of the Brown woman. He was just flirting, anyway, it was an ego thing. He knew he had a girl waiting.

Instead of taking the stairwell in the back, which was where the extras were supposed to exit, he went through the open doors that led to the interior of the production offices. He passed by a guy who may or may not have been security, and he said, "I'm about to use the bathroom," and the guy gave him a *Who cares?* expression. Rubin kept walking, down an open staircase to the first floor.

He passed by an art department, and a props area, people standing over draft tables and seated before large-screen computers, working, working...It was so foreign to him, how they did the same thing with diligence every day. He was impressed at their commitment and skill levels, but on the other hand he felt like that kind of drudgery would bore him to death, eventually. He liked not knowing what was coming next.

Rubin went by open-door offices, seeing middle-aged people who must be producers or some kind of production executives (they looked as tired as everyone else), and then he slowed down at a large office marked ACCOUNTING beside its door, where he saw several people at their desks, and one man, a rumpled-hair type wearing glasses, writing checks in a large book of them.

That's free money right there, thought Rubin. His blood ticked.

Out in the parking lot, he got into the Kia, hit the ignition, and waited. He looked around the lot, which was an interior space bordered on three sides by two other converted warehouses, now businesses.

One was a large workout club that seemed to be targeted at serious health freaks—young bodybuilders and hard trainers. Rubin had noticed the kinds of vehicles that were parked near its entrance: trucks elevated with

monster-sized wheels, tricked-out Wranglers and Bron-
cos, and loud-colored, hood-hemi Mopars, which fit the
profile of the clients.

The other business was a slightly used, scratch-and-
dent retail outfit whose very bare-bones appearance was
meant to suggest steep discounts. The sign over the loading platform read, CHARM CITY VALUELAND, and under-
neath, PUBLIC WELCOME. There was a double-front glass
door for customers and a single door, which looked to be
an employee entrance, on one side of the loading dock.
Rubin watched someone, a man with a company patch on
his shirt, come out of the employee entrance carrying a
padded freight package. He placed the package beside the
door and walked back into the warehouse.

Covid protocol, late stage, but it had stuck: Some
retailers were still putting their checks and accounting
paperwork outside their businesses for pickup.

What the hell, thought Rubin. *Why the fuck not?*

He looked at the buildings in the lot. He didn't see
any cameras. There probably *were* cameras, but he didn't
see them. He didn't *want* to see them. He put on a KN95
mask that he had in his pocket. Most people didn't wear
them outside now, but some did.

He let the car idle and got out of the car. He crossed
the lot with purpose. He took the concrete steps up onto
the loading dock of the Charm City Valueland outlet and
picked up the padded freight package. It had some weight.
He carried it to the Kia as if it was his, opened the back

door of the sedan, and pushed the package under the driver's seat, checking that it was secure.

He did not take note of a 2012, black, high-horse Jeep Cherokee that had entered the lot as he was walking back to the Kia, package in hand. Its driver slowed down as he checked Rubin out. The Jeep pulled into a space, but its driver did not exit the vehicle.

Rubin opened the front door of the Kia and got under the wheel. Presently, Jerrod Williams came out of the production offices and folded his tall frame into the passenger seat.

"We set?" said Williams.

"All good," said Rubin.

"Why you wearing that mask?"

"Habit."

Rubin removed the mask and pulled out of the lot. The driver of the Jeep had been using his iPhone to snap photos of Rubin, Williams, the Kia, and its plates.

————————

Darkness had fallen as they came out of the dank Baltimore Harbor Tunnel that ran under the Patapsco River. They emerged onto the mostly traffic-free, express stretch of 895 that would lead then to 95 South and D.C.

"How'd you like it?" said Williams. "You get the bug?"

"I don't think so," said Rubin. "Too much standing around."

"Actors wait. Sometimes they're in their trailers for

most of the day before they get called to set. And then they might only work for two hours or so. That's what it is."

"You always want to do this?"

"No, not always. Got the bug in high school."

"I get it. Like, in a school play. Where'd you go, Woodson? Eastern?"

"You're naming schools in the Northeast, like you think that's where I came up. Next thing you're gonna ask me is, did I play basketball."

"That's not unreasonable. You're what, six-four?"

"Six-five. And no, I didn't play ball. Don't assume."

"Where'd you go to high school, then?"

"Duke Ellington."

"The arts school?"

"Uh-huh. I didn't know what I wanted to do specifically, but I did know that I was interested in that side of things. Once I got in there, I fell in with the theater crowd. That school graduated some serious people, like Samira Wiley, the woman who played in *Orange Is the New Black*? Dave Chapelle came out of there, too. That trumpet player, Wallace Rooney..."

"What about you?"

"What do you mean?"

"You're in your thirties..."

"Not that it's any of your business, but people make their way in their own time. I came slow out of the blocks. That's all it is."

"What have you been doing all these years?"

"I went to college, for one. UDC, okay, but you know, it was college. And then I mostly worked in bookstores, because I liked to read. Truth is, I was a heavy weed smoker, man. And so the time just passed. I did a lot of dreaming about becoming an actor, and then one day I realized that when I was up on tree I was *only* dreaming. I wasn't doing anything *about* those dreams. Now I'm on it."

"I guess that gun charge got in your way, too."

"You don't know me."

"I'm just saying…"

"Before that day, I had never been in trouble with the law, ever, in my life. I was riding in Southeast with my cousin Donald, we were going to see our aunt, still lives in Washington Highlands. Donald didn't make a full stop at a four-way, and we got pulled over. *Po*lice used that 'smell of marijuana' excuse to embolden themselves to search the vehicle. Donald had a thing under the seat. I didn't even know."

"An illegal handgun."

"They're *all* illegal in the District, unless you jump through all kinds of hoops and get some kind of special license. Thing that made this a real problem was, Donald's gun had no numbers. He bought it secondhand, and that's how it came to him…Shaved numbers, that right there will get you *all* jammed up with the law."

"Why'd he have a gun to begin with?"

"Same reason most people own guns in D.C. Donald is no gangster. He wanted a gun for protection. Used to be, if you weren't in the life, you didn't have to worry about such things. But now, out here, you get carjacked, you get robbed at gunpoint just pumping gas into your car...People are scared."

"Well, you got off. And I suppose you learned."

"I learned not to get in a car with someone less I know what's in the car. That's what I learned."

"Right," said Rubin, with a touch of guilt, thinking of the package under his seat. "What's your plan? Like, how are you gonna get to the next level?"

"Well, I don't have an agent. That's a chicken-egg thing. I've got a friend who was on a limited series, and he gave me the name of the lady in New York who cast him. I got through to her. Actually, it was her assistant. So now, hopefully, I'm on her radar screen. I did a couple of local commercials. No lines, but it helps me with my credits. And I been pestering the woman who does all the local casting for shows in Baltimore, her spot's in Canton, in the Broom Factory. She says she's going to let me audition for a series that's coming to town. Not a lead, mind you, those get cast in New York and Los Angeles. But a recurring part. These shows cast the supporting parts locally so they don't have to travel and house the actors."

"Sounds like you're making progress."

"I'm trying."

Rubin dropped Williams off at his place, an apartment he shared with two other men, in a complex steps away from the Rhode Island Avenue Metro stop. Williams asked for Rubin's phone, and when Rubin handed it over to him, Williams entered his digits into the phone.

"I'm working that courtroom scene in a couple of days. If you get called for it, text me. We can ride up to Baltimore together, if that's okay with you."

"Sure."

"Thanks, Ira."

Williams got out of the car and walked down the street. He didn't go into any of the entrances on that particular block. Maybe he was waiting for Rubin to drive away. He was being careful, which was understandable. Still, Williams had called him Ira for the first time. Rubin felt good about that.

———————

That night, Rubin waited for Maria to get in the shower before he opened the package. He was hoping to find cash, though he knew that was improbable, and indeed there was no folding money in the mix. There were checks, though, all made out to Charm City Valueland, he surmised from customers or from employees buying goods at a reduced rate. There was also paperwork enumerating the pending deposits of the checks. He found a few checks that he thought he might try to cash, those that were almost illegible on the *Pay to the Order of* line. Finally, as Maria's shower was surely winding down, he quickly separated the checks that were to be drawn from LTI, a national chain of banks that had recently come to the East Coast from California and opened multiple branches in the DMV and in Baltimore. Rubin had a plan.

Soon after he stashed the package under their bedroom dresser, Maria came into the room, rubbing a towel through her hair. She was wrapped in a bathrobe.

"Hey," said Rubin. "What are we doing tonight?"

"Linda's out."

"Thank you, God."

"So we can order a Ledo's pizza and watch a movie or something."

"Can I watch you get dressed first?"

"If you'd like."

"Thank you," said Rubin. He thought of the cash that would soon be lining his pockets. "Let's go out tomorrow night. I'll make sure it's nice."

———————

The next day was a full one for Rubin. After Maria walked to her classes at Montgomery College, Rubin set out to try and cash a few checks, all of them less than a thousand dollars. He went to three branches of LTI and on the third, in Brookland, Northeast, he was successful. Most of the time he was asked for ID, and he'd simply say that he had forgotten it that morning, but in the Brookland branch the bored teller did not ask him for one. Rubin had endorsed the check with chicken scratch, as the original check-writer had done, and walked out of the bank with $439.19 in hand.

He wore his mask in all of the banks. That was not unusual; many of the patrons still wore masks, and it would make his identification much harder later on, as surely he had been captured on camera. But Rubin knew the basic truth that the general public did not know: the law did not aggressively pursue check fraud, unless the perpetrator hit the banks repeatedly and too hard. Law enforcement had bigger problems to solve. They simply did not have the resources or the time to pursue pocket-change fraudsters like Ira Rubin.

Rubin drove to an office-supply chain store and purchased a box of perforated, premium check stock paper that had the added security feature of watermarks.

His next stop was on Georgia Avenue, in North Petworth, west of Sherman Circle. He knew a guy who lived above a Salvadoran restaurant there on the commercial strip. His name was Louis Ellis, a white dude married to a Black woman. They had two children, and the family stayed in this spacious apartment on The Avenue. Some of his acquaintances called him Doc, in honor of Dock Ellis, who pitched a no-hitter for the Pittsburgh Pirates in 1970 while tripping his ass off on LSD. None of them were old enough to remember that event, but Dock Ellis's legend had endured.

"All alone today?" said Rubin, after Ellis had let him into his spot. There were toys spread about the cluttered room, and Pokémon cards scattered on the living-room rug.

"The kids are at school or day care," said Ellis. "Wanda is at work."

"You're off?"

"Ha," said Ellis. "What can I do for you, Ira? Would you like to purchase some smoke?" Ellis's core business was weed.

"You know that's not me. I got something else in mind."

Ellis owned the software for formatting checks. He owned a laser printer. He had magnetic ink and the MICR font to reproduce the computer-friendly numbers at the bottom of each check.

"This is the one," said Rubin, passing over the check he had chosen from the package he had stolen. It was from a man (Rubin would not "do this" to a woman, his idea of chivalry) whose bank was a well-known chain with branches nationwide.

"How many do you need?" said Ellis.

"Run all of these," said Rubin, handing Ellis the box of check formatting paper.

"What's our deal?"

"I'm going to give you a hundred right now for your time," said Rubin. "Then, you're gonna get twenty percent of what I earn."

"That's generous," said Ellis, shaking his white-boy dreads away from his face. "But how are we gonna, you know, *account* for what's owed?"

"You know me," said Rubin. "I wouldn't fuck you, Doc."

"Give me a couple of days," said Ellis.

Rubin peeled off five twenties from his roll.

On the way home, Rubin stopped at a small store in Takoma Park that sold beautiful, unusual jewelry, and bought a necklace of precious gemstones encased in sterling silver. The Turkish woman who owned the store wrapped it for him with care. He paid her in cash from his ill-gotten earnings.

That night, Rubin took Maria to La Tomate, the venerable restaurant and social spot set on the V-shaped corner of Connecticut and R, in Dupont Circle. They first split a calamari salad, then Rubin had the Bolognese over linguini, while Maria went with the branzino fillet. They shared an actual bottle of Super Tuscany wine, rather than a carafe of the house red, and ordered Fonseca Vintage port with their dessert, a sorbetti assortment.

Maria was wearing her necklace. The wrapping and box were on the table. It was perfect on her. Rubin knew it would be.

"You're beautiful," said Rubin.

"You're so good to me, Ira."

He said, "I want to be."

Later, in the bedroom of her apartment, they made it last. When they kissed it was as if they were made for it. Rubin could not believe his good fortune. And then, after, when they lay naked atop the sheets, her chest glistening with beads of sweat in the light of the pedestal candle she had placed on her nightstand, she was still wearing the necklace. He had asked her to keep it on.

"This was a good night," said Rubin.

"Yes."

"I hope we didn't bother Linda. You were pretty loud."

"*You* were."

"I was praying."

"Is that what you meant when you shouted 'God'?"

"Linda hates me. Did you see her mean-mugging me when we came home?"

"No, but I don't doubt it."

"Linda doesn't like men? Is that it?"

"Don't be a pig. She doesn't like *you*."

"But why?"

"Linda respects the law, and you don't. I'm saying, you haven't in the past. See, Linda's father is police, here in the District. Started out in uniform, like they do, and worked himself up to Detective. Her father is her hero, as fathers should be. He taught her self-defense. He taught her how to shoot."

"Now I'm getting worried."

"I'll protect you, Cariño," said Maria, and she kissed him on the cheek. "Are you working anymore this week?"

"Mañana," said Rubin, getting into the spirit. "I got texted by the woman in charge of extras. I'm going up to Baltimore in the morning, taking my friend Jerrod with me. I'll need your car again. I hope that's all right…"

"Yeah, sure. It's good that you are working. Do you like this job?"

"It's okay. It's nothing that I'm serious about. I mean, nothing is really serious in the scheme of things, right?"

He was holding her and looking up at the ceiling, where she had stuck many fluorescent stars. They were glowing now, as if they were floating in the night sky. It was something that parents would do for a child, in a child's room, only Maria wasn't childlike. She was a serious young woman who had ambition and still cared to dream. Rubin had no ambition, and he had long stopped dreaming of another path.

"What do you mean, in the scheme of things?" said Maria.

"Well, given what we all know about life, about how it ends…" Rubin stroked her bare arm. "I had this uncle. Uncle Irving. My father's brother. Irv was kind of a…I'd call him a free spirit, stuck in time. He came of age in the '60s, but none of that revolution or hippie stuff wore off on him. He looked like a singer you'd see at The Sands in Vegas. Black hair, wore it high and oiled. Listened to a lot of Sinatra, fell in love with women at the drop of a hat. He was a romantic. Never could hold a job in his life, but, happy. You know?"

"I think so."

"Anyway. When I was younger, my parents used to ask me what my plans were for the future. Uncle Irv would say to me, 'Don't worry about it, kid—nothing really matters in this life. You work your tail off for the corner office, to buy the car with the certain badge, to pay the dues at the country club, to wear the right watch…and for what? Our time here on earth, it's nothing but an amusement machine. You get on the ride for as long as it lasts, and you have fun, and then you get off. You've had your turn. Then you walk away from the carnival park, and as you keep walking, the lights from the park fade and it begins to get dark. You can't see anyone, and they can't see you. And then you're in darkness, forever. You're forgotten. You can own a mansion or live on the streets, drive a Mercedes-Benz or have no car at all. Everyone goes to the same place. Darkness. So there's no reason to waste your precious time striving for status or possessions. It doesn't matter. Nothing does.'"

"I don't believe that," said Maria. "I am going to graduate from college and go on to nursing school. I'll have a house someday. Children and grandchildren."

"For what? Don't you see?"

"No, I don't see. You scare me sometimes, Ira."

"I don't mean to. It's just the way I feel."

He fell asleep first. She listened to his heavy breathing and stared at the stars on the ceiling. After a while she worked her arm out from under him, turned on her side, and closed her eyes.

———————

Rubin, Williams, a couple of dozen extras, and the film crew were in a replica of a courtroom that had been built on the stages near the production offices in East Baltimore. Rubin was in the gallery, seated with other background who were supposed to be spectators. The crew was setting up the shot. It looked like an actual courtroom, and was lit to suggest the time of day in which the "trial" would occur.

Remarkable, thought Rubin. *All these people, doing their jobs, craftsmen and craftswomen, artists in their own way, all of them.*

If only he had gotten interested in this kind of thing when he was younger. And then he thought, *I'd get bored with it eventually.*

The director, a Black man in an LA Dodgers baseball cap, no older than Rubin, had come out of video village, where he typically sat before monitors with the DP and Script Supervisor. He looked around the courtroom and studied the extras. The director said something quietly to the Second-Second AD, Ras Mike, who then came over to Jerrod Williams and told him to move over to the jury box, where he replaced one of the other extras seated there. Ras Mike produced a copy of the "sides"—a paper version of the scripted scenes that were to be shot that day—and pointed out something to Williams. Rubin could not hear the conversation, but he surmised that Williams had been given a line.

Rubin saw Williams smile, then begin to mouth words to himself. He looked amped.

The master was shot first. The scene was five pages long, unusual for any script, with several lengthy monologues involving witnesses on the stand. There was much coverage to be done and this would be the only scene scheduled for the day.

As the A and B cameras rolled, the actor playing the judge asked the question, "Has the jury come to a verdict?" Williams stood and said, "We have, Your Honor."

Williams said his line multiple times over the course of the day. His delivery got stronger as the camera moved in on him. He was "saving it" for his close-up. He had thought it out.

Rubin was happy for his friend.

At the end of the day, Rubin sat in the parking lot of the production offices behind the wheel of the idling Kia, waiting for Williams, who had been the last to turn in his costume. He had rolled down his window to get some air.

Williams came out of the offices, a spring in his step. He spotted the Kia, walked to it, opened the door, and dropped into the passenger seat.

"Congratulations," said Rubin.

"Big day for me," said Williams.

"You get paid above the rate when you have a line, right?"

"I think it's eight hundred dollars, something like that. Plus residuals. But that's not even the point, Ira, it's not about the money. I got a *speaking* part. I'm on my way."

Rubin heard footsteps on pavement and looked in his side-view mirror. A man was coming up alongside their vehicle. Before he had time to register the situation, the man was leaning into the driver's window. He had produced a revolver and he pressed its muzzle with aggression into the flesh behind Rubin's ear.

"Don't say nothin," said the man. He stank of

perspiration. His lank hair touched his shoulders and he had a long beard. "Move funny and I'll use this."

"We don't have any money," said Rubin, the stability in his own voice surprising him. "Neither of us do."

"Told you not to speak. I'm going to get in the back seat and we're going to take a drive. Don't do something stupid and try to take off without me. Unlock my door."

Rubin hit a button. All of the doors unlocked. Quickly, the man, Robert Taylor, who went by RT, got into the back seat of the Kia and shut the door.

"Drive this Korean piece of shit," said Taylor. "I'll tell you where."

They left the lot. It was a short drive. Rubin and Williams were silent as Taylor directed them to an isolated area under the stretch of O'Donnell Street that bridged the railroad tracks. He told them to park beside a thick concrete support pile that was off the road. Rubin noticed that Williams had laced his fingers together in his lap to steady his hands.

"Let it run," said Taylor. "Now I'll cut to the chase. You stole something the other day. I'm speaking to you, Pedro. Or Ach-med. Whatever you are."

Rubin knew that the long-bearded man was talking to him. He looked into the rearview mirror. The man was white, his blue eyes pink and watery. He was holding the gun low, still pointed at Rubin.

"He wasn't involved," said Rubin, evenly, making a slight nod toward Williams. "He's got nothing to do with this."

"I don't care," said Taylor.

"Look, if you had a check in that package, I apologize," said Rubin. "I didn't know—"

"I didn't have any check in that package, Slick. I had *eyes* on that package. I'd been scoping that situation out. The day you stole it was the day I was about to get it my *own* self."

"I'll give it to you," said Rubin. "All of it."

"I know you will. But I'm gonna use this situation we got to my advantage. I'm gonna let you do my work for me. So what I want you to do is, I want you to take one of those checks, pick one from one of the big banks, and make me some blanks. Get yourself some check paper and a laser printer—"

"I know how to do it," said Rubin.

"Say it again?"

"I'll *do* it," said Rubin. "I know how it's done."

He didn't tell Taylor that it was already in the works.

"Okay. How long?"

"I'll need a couple of days."

"Ain't no couple of days about it," said Taylor. "It'll be tomorrow night. Now give me your phones. The both of you. Come on."

Rubin and Williams handed their phones over the back seat. Taylor took them and got to work. On Rubin's phone, in the home screen of the Settings file, Taylor got Rubin's name and cell number. In the Favorites file, he found the Home notation, and there he obtained the address of the apartment Rubin shared with Maria.

Taylor made screenshots of all of this and sent them to his own phone. The tall Black man in the passenger seat had been more careful; he had wisely entered his name but not his home address into his own phone. Taylor didn't need it. He owned the thief. Taylor returned their phones to them.

"Drive me back," said Taylor.

They stopped in the lot of the production offices. Taylor slipped the revolver into his jacket pocket.

"I'll text you, *Ira*," said Taylor. "I know you won't go to the law, because you'd be putting yourself in for this, too. But don't even bother to have my number traced. The phone I'll be texting you from is a throwaway."

"I'll wait for your text," said Rubin.

"Remember, I know where you live," said Taylor. "When I get out this car, drive."

Taylor stepped out of the car and closed its door. Rubin drove off the lot. He didn't look in the mirrors to see where Taylor was headed. He only wanted to get away.

———————

"You're a low person," said Williams, quietly, as they neared the Harbor Tunnel.

"I'm sorry," said Rubin.

"Knew I shouldn't have got involved with you. I *knew*. Stupid, man. *Stupid*."

"I'm sorry, Jerrod."

"Don't speak to me."

The rest of the trip was spent in silence. As they neared the Rhode Island Avenue Metro station, the street crowded with pedestrians, Williams said, "I'll get out here."

"I can drive you to your door."

Williams didn't look at Rubin. "I don't want you to know where I live."

Williams got out of the car and walked down the block, toward the apartments. Rubin drove home.

The next day, Rubin was scheduled to work for Maria's cousin Julito on the landscaping gig, but he didn't show up. He didn't call Julito to give him a bullshit excuse. Rubin was preoccupied.

He phoned Doc Ellis, who told Rubin that he had gotten busy with wife-and-children matters, and that the checks were not yet done. Ellis promised Rubin that the checks would be ready the next day.

Rubin got a call from Julito but he let it go to message.

Late in the day, he received a text from the man with the long beard. It was only a question mark. Rubin replied, Tomorrow. The man replied, No, tonight. Rubin blocked the text number and shut off his phone.

Maria came home from school. She said to him, "How was work with Julito today?" and he said, "It went fine."

Her eyes said she knew he was lying. She must have gotten a call from her cousin, asking why her boyfriend had not shown up for work. But she didn't confront him. The look of disappointment on her face was worse than an accusation.

Midevening, Linda Rodriguez entered the apartment. Rubin and Maria were on the couch, watching a television show about British royalty that Maria had chosen and Rubin was tolerating. Linda didn't look at Rubin. She said to Maria, "I just ordered some food for delivery, Maria. It's paid for and tipped out. When it comes, will you bring it inside?"

"Sure," said Maria.

"I'll be in my room."

Linda drifted. A few minutes later, there was a knock on the door.

"That was fast," said Maria.

"I'll get it," said Rubin.

He went to the door, turned the knob. The man with the long beard pushed on the door violently. Rubin stumbled back. Taylor walked in, closing the door behind him. Maria screamed.

"Shut your mouth," said Taylor to Maria. To Rubin he pointed and said, "*You.*"

Taylor rushed Rubin, gathered his shirt up in his fists, and danced Rubin back until he hit the wall. Maria froze, unable to speak.

Taylor, up in Rubin's face, said, "I told you, *tonight.* Where is it?"

"I won't have it until tomorrow," said Rubin.

"That wasn't our deal."

The rack of a slide silenced the room.

"Hands up," said Linda Rodriguez. "I have a gun. I'm pointing it at the back of your head."

"Easy, lady," said Taylor. He released his grip on Rubin and raised his hands.

"Don't move and don't speak," said Linda. She was three feet away from him. The gun, a Glock 17, the same MPD service weapon that her father had trained her on, the one that she had become proficient with at area ranges, now had a live round in the chamber. The safety was off.

"You gonna shoot someone in here?"

"I would."

"I'm not even armed."

"You're an intruder. I have another gun in my bedroom. After I shoot you, I'll put the throw-down in your cold hand."

"Jesus. All right."

"Turn around and walk out of here. Keep your eyes on the floor and your hands up until you reach the door. Don't look back or say anything. Go ahead."

Taylor did as he was told. But he did mutter, "Tomorrow," before he left.

"Thank you," said Rubin to Linda. And: "I'm sorry."

Linda turned to Maria. "I want this fucking lowlife out of my apartment."

Linda safetied her weapon and walked back into her room, shutting the door behind her.

"Maria…"

"You need to go," said Maria, dry-eyed and resolute.

"You bring this to where we live? You lie to me? You screw my cousin Julito, which you promised you would never do? Ira, I don't want you here anymore."

"Okay," said Rubin. "Okay. Let me get my things. But tomorrow, can I borrow your car?"

"*Ira.*"

"Just one more time."

There was a knock on the front door. A muffled voice behind the door said, "Food delivery."

Maria crossed her arms tightly across her chest. Rubin shrugged.

As hurt as Maria was, she was not the type to put Rubin out on the street, so she let him spend the night behind the closed door of her bedroom. In the morning, when he was certain that Linda Rodriguez had left for work, Rubin gathered his things, which consisted of some clothing, his shaving kit, and the original shipping package with the remaining checks, still stashed under Maria's dresser. Maria was not about to loan Rubin her Kia, but she did drive him to a small rental-car outfit on Sligo Avenue in Silver Spring. She had to use her credit card to rent a compact car for him, as he was without one and the business wouldn't accept cash. Rubin vowed to pay her back, a promise that Maria knew he'd never keep.

"You're a good person," said Rubin. "I'm sorry for everything. I don't deserve you."

Maria did not disagree. Rubin tried to kiss her on the mouth but she gave him her cheek.

He drove the rental, a Nissan Something-Or-Other, down to Doc Ellis's apartment, where he picked up the blank checks. They looked real. Rubin didn't have the heart to tell Ellis there would be no future earnings.

Rubin texted Taylor and told him he was ready to meet. Taylor's reply text read, Under O'Donnell Street, same spot.

Rubin drove to Baltimore, parked idling by the concrete pile supporting the bridge. It was an overcast day of light, steady rain.

Fifteen minutes later Taylor's black Jeep approached. As it neared him, Rubin read its Maryland license-plate number and punched the letters and numbers into the Notes app of his iPhone, balanced on his leg.

Taylor pulled alongside him, his window down, the vehicles nose to ass, police-style. Taylor was wearing the same jacket from the night before and there were crumbs in his beard.

Rubin passed the freight package through the open windows. Taylor opened it, examined the contents. He didn't comment beyond a satisfied nod.

"We good?" said Rubin.

"Let me remind you of something. If you were to go to the law with any of this, you'd be in a whole world of trouble. You committed a rack of serious crimes here. If anyone with a badge comes calling on me, I'll put you in for it. Your tall dark friend, too."

"I have no doubt."

After Taylor drove away, Rubin went directly to Baltimore's Eastern District Police Station on Edison Highway. He entered the station house and spoke to the desk sergeant.

"I want to report a kidnapping," said Rubin.

After a while a uniformed officer came out to the lobby and spoke to Rubin. Rubin gave the uniformed officer a few more details and was told to wait where he sat. Soon a middle-aged detective wearing a sport jacket and tie appeared. Rubin was screened, then led back to a small room, where he and the detective sat at a table. There was a yellow notebook pad on the table along with a pen.

"You say you were kidnapped," said the detective, dubiously. His name was Ross.

"Yes. The kidnapper had a gun, I don't know what kind. It was a revolver. I have the license-plate number of his vehicle. I don't know his name."

"Can you tell me why you were taken?" said Ross, looking Rubin over. "Was it, like, a ransom situation?"

"I stole a freight package of checks that were left outside a retail store off Ponca Street. A place called Charm City Valueland. The man who kidnapped me had intended to steal the checks himself, so he jacked me up."

Ross had been taking notes. He laid the pen down on the pad.

"You realize," said Ross, "you're going to be charged for the theft."

"Yes, I know."

When Robert Taylor was arrested without incident,

he gave the police the names of Ira Rubin and Jerrod Williams. Upon questioning, Rubin told the law that Williams, though he too had been kidnapped, had not been involved in the theft and had no knowledge of it at the time that Rubin had committed the crime. A Charm City Valueland camera, mounted on the building (yes, there had been a camera), had shown a masked, average-sized white man walking across the parking lot, package in hand, to his car, a compact import, license plate obscured. Shortly thereafter, a tall Black man, Jerrod Williams, emerged from the on-site production offices of a television show and got into the same car with Rubin. Williams, when picked up and questioned, denied any knowledge of the theft at the time of its commission, saying that he learned about it only two days later, when he was taken by a man, at gunpoint, for a ride. The police officer who interviewed Williams believed him, and in any case there was insufficient evidence to charge him with a crime. He was more valuable as a witness, and, deemed credible, he testified at the trial of Robert Taylor, who had multiple priors. Taylor took a long fall.

Rubin was given an eighteen-month sentence for his crimes due to the egregious violation of the terms of his probation. He did a year of soft time at the Central Maryland Correctional Facility in Sykesville, a minimum security unit. There he worked in the Central Laundry, which processed clothing and towels for numerous other correctional institutions in the state. His father visited him twice a month on Tuesdays.

Ira Rubin came out with a little more weight on him. His hair was flecked with gray. His beard, when he went unshaved for a couple of days, had gray in it as well.

He was less cocky than he had been in the past. The rooster had lost its strut.

He was living, "temporarily" he said, in his parents' house in Barnaby Woods, on the D.C. side of Chevy Chase. He stayed in his old bedroom, which, thankfully, his folks had converted into a guest room, absent of any evidence of his youth. He was thirty-four years old.

One day he walked outside and talked to the owner of a landscaping business whose crew serviced the houses in the neighborhood. The owner, Odell, was a stout Latino fellow wearing a curly-*W* baseball cap. He worked alongside his crew. Rubin introduced himself and asked Odell if he had any openings.

"You serious?" said Odell.

"Very," said Rubin. "I had a job on a crew a couple of years ago. I was on the blower. I'm motivated. I won't let you down."

"Well..." said Odell. Rubin's parents had been clients for a couple of years, and they had been good to him. "Sometimes my guys don't show up. Give me your phone number. Maybe I let you pick up a day here and there."

The work was sporadic, at best. Rubin got with the crew two times over the course of the next month. But it was a fortuitous connection. At a work picnic thrown by

Odell, he met a young Nicaraguan named Bianca, dark, compact, and shapely (his type), with a sly sense of humor (also compulsory). Rubin, though now a bit long in the tooth, still had charm and he worked it well.

In the meantime, one of the do-gooder, reentry outfits in the District offered to help him find a job. When he told the nice earnest woman his interests, she made a phone call for him. He interviewed at the AFI Theater and was given a part-time position as a ticket-taker there in the lobby.

Bianca lived with her extended family in a spacious, ramshackle bungalow in Manor Park, Northwest. Her room was in the basement, where others in the family shared a downstairs kitchen. Upstairs lived the matriarch—Bianca's grandmother, Almara—a tiny unsmiling woman who ran a catering business out of the house and used no English, if she knew any at all. There were many adults and children living there, some blood-related, some not, and three small dogs. Religious imagery was prevalent on the walls. Almara the matriarch was a devout Catholic.

Rubin and Bianca's relationship had deepened and he moved into the house. A handsome and fit young Nicaraguan named Max, who lived in the basement with another granddaughter and their toddler son, was an independent contractor, and when he wasn't on a paid job he built creative play equipment in the backyard for the children, and coops for chickens, who supplied Almara with eggs.

Max and Rubin became friendly. Max taught Rubin

rudimentary carpentry and took him along as an occasional helper on jobs. On the weekends, there were parties at night in the yard with music, and Christmas lights strung between the trees. The dogs and children chased the chickens but did not harm them.

At the AFI Theater, the manager allowed Rubin to introduce some of the old black-and-white films when they ran. On those nights, Bianca came and sat in the auditorium. He missed her terribly when she was at her job in a nail salon. For Rubin, it was a happy time.

It's hard to say, exactly, why he couldn't manage to make it last.

If he had been asked, Rubin would have said that he only wanted to buy Bianca something nice, a piece of jewelry that would symbolize their bond. He'd take her out to dinner, something better than fast casual, where he would give her the present, as he had done with Maria. But he was broke and he needed to fund his plans. So he enlisted Ellis to print some blank checks, who had bet unwisely, once again, on the promised income. Then Rubin went to a bank and successfully cashed one of the checks. And then he went to a second bank and covered the first with another check. This worked, so he tried it again. And again. He got greedy, and the last check he wrote was for over ten thousand dollars. This put him in the gunsights of the Feds.

He was arrested and charged with felony fraud.

Ira Rubin sat in one of the interview rooms in the D.C.
Jail, across the table from his father, Phillip Rubin, who
had come to visit him.

Phil Rubin wore a sport coat that he had purchased
from his salesman at the Saks in Chevy Chase, a dapper,
cool fellow named Chauncy. He wore a Rolex Explorer,
the basic model, on his wrist. Phil looked prosperous, and
he was, but it was not overdone. His head of silver-gray
hair was full, and his Sephardic skin tone gave him the
appearance of being perpetually tanned. He was a six
footer, two inches taller than Ira. Phil often wondered if
that height difference, and his own success, was part of
Ira's "problem." In a complicated way, it's not good for a
man to be more than his son.

Phil had made his money in commercial real estate.
His father, Ira's grandfather, Murray Rubin, had owned
a small corner market on Euclid Street in Columbia
Heights, Northwest. Like many Jews, Greeks, and Ital-
ians who owned small businesses, Murray had "bought
the building," which had ensured a healthy retirement for
him and his wife, and a nice inheritance for his two sons,
Phillip and Irving. Phil had repeatedly told his own sons,
"Buy the real estate. Do you know why they call it that?
Cash isn't real. The stock market isn't real. Only dirt is
real. It's the financial foundation." Like practically every
bit of wisdom that Phil had tried to impart to him, Ira
hadn't listened.

"Was it a long wait to get in?" said Rubin.

"Always," said Phil. "It's like going through the

airport, magnified. A lady guard was even hand-searching a nun when I arrived. It's an indignity, but I don't mind. I like visiting you."

"You do?"

"Yes."

"But you're busy."

"Not too busy for you."

Phil was seventy but not retired. He had no plans to step back. He had properties to manage and protect.

"Your mother sends her love," said Phil. "It's too upsetting for her to come here. I hope you understand."

"I do."

"What does your lawyer say?" Phil had hired one with a good reputation, recommended by the family's tax attorney.

"My trial's coming up. I'll probably get a couple of years, Federal time. They can send me anywhere in the country. But my lawyer is going to ask for a facility in Maryland or Virginia. Who knows if the judge will go along with it? But hopefully I won't be too far away from you and Mom. Or Bianca."

"She's still by your side?"

"Yes. She visits me regularly. She's supportive...like you."

"I spoke to Odell last week," said Phil. "He asked after you. He said you did a good job for him on the landscaping crew, the few times he used you."

"I tried."

"How about your position at the movie theater? Do you think they'll have you back?"

"I'll contact them when I come home. I guess I'll have to see."

"You always liked those black-and-white movies."

"That came from Uncle Irving. He was into that old stuff."

"He was a dreamer. He thought those movies were real."

"Uncle Irv was a character," said Rubin.

"He was a bum," said Phil, his eyes narrowing. "And you looked up to him."

"Irv was happy. There's nothing wrong with that, is there?"

"His stories," said Phil, with disdain. "Always with the Ferris wheels and merry-go-rounds…"

"He called them amusement machines."

"Imagine basing your whole life philosophy on a bull-shit story like that. 'We're all going to die, so what's the point of working?' It's an excuse to lead a rudderless life. And you bought into it."

Rubin said nothing.

"Your Uncle Irv was a gonif," said Phil. "A loser who left corpses in his wake. He married a sweet girl who had his babies and then he proceeded to fuck everything with a pulse. All of his cheap girlfriends. Do you know that Irving stole from your grandfather, our own father? That's right—he plundered the register of the market on Euclid Street one day, just so he could finance a trip to

Atlantic City with one of his whores. Irv couldn't keep his shvantz in his pants to save his life. And you think he was happy. Do you know how he ended up?"

"He died in a nursing home," said Rubin.

"Broke. I paid for his care. The last two years he wore a colostomy bag. He walked around with a bag of shit on his hip, and not even his children came to visit him. Only me. He was alone. To *him* you looked up."

"No," said Rubin. "I looked up to you, Dad. But you never had faith in me."

"Please," said Phil. "I made mistakes like all parents do, but I always supported you. Look at your life. I had faith in you. I still do. I'm sitting here, *right here*."

"I'm…"

"Don't do that. Don't say you're sorry. *Prove* you're sorry, Ira. When you get out…for God's sake, do something right."

His father had grown agitated. Rubin stayed silent and allowed him to settle.

"Listen," said Phil, sitting back in his chair. "I have something to tell you. My father used to say to me, 'No matter what your children do, no matter how much they disappoint you, treat them equally in the end. You have two children, it should be two equal shares. To the penny. It's more than a mitzvah—it's simply the right thing to do.'"

"What are you saying, Dad?"

"Your mother and I have more money than we can ever spend. At this point we're living on the interest. Our house is worth a bundle and our savings are substantial. When we pass…"

"You all are not going anywhere just yet."

"When we *pass*, Ira…you and your brother are going to inherit a great deal of money. Millions. Do you understand?"

Ira Rubin nodded, looking down at the table. He should have been happy. He'd never felt so ashamed.

"But I don't want you to just *wait* for it," said Phil. "The day you come out, this time, is day one. A fresh start."

"Yes, sir."

"I know you can do it."

Phil reached across the table and placed his hand over Rubin's.

"I love you, son."

"I love *you*."

———

A couple of weeks later, Rubin was in the chapel with other inmates, waiting for the day's speaker to arrive. Danielle the librarian's book club had morphed into a succession of random speakers meant to motivate the incarcerated. A kind of Career Day for men who lived in cells and could not go to work.

Jerrod Williams entered the chapel, accompanied by a guard. Rubin saw him and smiled. He knew he was coming, he'd seen his name on the jailhouse flyer.

Williams was wearing a nice sweater, tailored slacks, and a fresh pair of Adidas Ultraboost. He was cleanly dressed but not showy.

Up at the lectern, Williams said, "My name is Jerrod Williams, and I'm an actor."

He talked about his road and his craft. He talked about how to get there. Like anything worthwhile, he said, it involved hard work.

The men had heard this many times before. They had also listened to multiple speakers who had used variations of *You can be anything you set your mind to*. They were anxious to get to the question-and-answer portion of the talk. They wanted to know how much money he made and did he get much play.

"I make a decent living," said Williams. "But I would do this no matter what they paid me."

"You get extra when they do reruns?" asked a man.

"It's called residuals. Actors live off of residuals. I'm lucky because this show I'm on now, *Forensics: Baltimore*, is what they call an episodic show, instead of one long story every season. It means the episodes stand alone, they begin and end with a resolution. So they can go to syndication, which are reruns on another network, and they can run them on a loop, out of sequence, the way they do with those *Law and Order* shows. That's how actors make real coin."

"I saw that Baltimore show in the dayroom," said a man. "And I saw you *in* it. You play, like, a technician in the morgue, right? Why you always sitting down?"

"It's what my character would be doing," said Williams. "He works in front of a laptop. But also, I'm very tall, as you can see. The producers don't want me to be towering over the lead actors. So they generally shoot me sitting down."

"You're tall as *mess*. You play basketball?"

"No."

"You trying to be like Denzel or Jamie Foxx?"

"I don't think so," said Williams. "Those guys have a quality…they're movie stars, and they're good actors. I'm more of a supporting actor, and I'm good with that. I'd like to be known as a character actor, eventually. But all I want in the end is to leave a mark."

"Can you elaborate on that?" said Rubin.

Williams looked at Rubin and nodded. "Sure. I think an artist…if you all will allow me to call myself that…is hyper-aware of his mortality. I mean, we all understand that we're going to die someday. But an artist spits in the face of that reality. Fifty years from now, most likely I'll be gone, but maybe somebody will be watching an old thing I did and say, 'Oh yeah, that's that tall brother who used to play on those shows.' It's like a long-dead writer whose name is on the spine of a chapter book in a library. His name on that book…it proves that he was here. It means he existed. You know?"

Some of the men nodded. The room was quiet, but the atmosphere was not somber. They were thinking.

"I bet you *get* some, though," said a man, and many of the others chuckled and relaxed.

"I have a girlfriend," said Williams. "She's an actress here in town."

Afterward, when Danielle told the men that the session was done, some gathered around Williams to say a few words and shake his hand. Rubin stayed back, and when the others had gone, he approached Williams. The guard would be telling him to move along shortly, and he knew he didn't have much time.

"Hey."

"Ira. Sorry to see you back inside."

"Yeah, you know. Hopefully this is it, for me. I'm looking at a couple of years."

"What are you going to do when you come out?"

"I don't know. I was starting to do a little contracting when I got arrested. Home-renovation stuff. A guy named Max took me under his wing. I kinda liked it."

"Contact me," said Williams. "I assume you still have my number in your phone. This job I'm on, it's got a five-season guarantee from Paramount Plus. The showrunner is their golden boy, so the network is giving him everything he wants. You remember Ras Mike?"

"Light-skinned guy with dreads?"

"He's on the show. He'll put you on if I ask him to."

"He'll hire someone like me?"

"We got all kinds of people on the crew who did time, some for more serious shit than you've ever been involved in. You'd have to start as a Production Assistant, like everyone else. It's a tough job, but from there you could make some contacts with the crew, maybe move into set construction, something like that."

"Thanks, man. I mean, *Jerrod*."

"Always clowning."

"I appreciate you. For real."

Rubin extended his hand. Williams shook it.

———————

As he exited the facility, Jerrod Williams breathed deeply of the free air.

That night, he and his girlfriend, Tracey, a working actress in the D.C. theater world, ordered dinner in to their small apartment in Shaw. Williams had a scene up in the morning, and he had printed two copies of the sides. As they waited for their food to arrive, they sat on the couch together, their legs touching, and read lines.

THE NO-KNOCK

HE'D BEEN AWAKE for forty-five minutes, drinking his first cup of coffee, working his way through the morning paper, as he did every morning, methodically. He had gotten up out of his reading chair to refill his cup. As he came to the front door of his house, he looked outside, hearing the sound of vehicles bouncing into his driveway, high-rev engines, brakes locking in, tires skidding to a stop. He saw two black windowless vans, their side doors sliding open, and men emerging from the open doors wearing black uniforms, Kevlar, sidearms holstered. They carried semiautomatic rifles, a couple of them holding battering rams, all of them now running toward his home, a few going under the front porch to the basement door, others coming up the stairs to the porch itself. *I know what this is*, thought Joseph Caruso. And then he thought: *Vince*.

Caruso turned his head, looked back into the family room where his wife, Angie, sat on the couch with their daughter, Gianna, watching TV. The Carusos' two dogs, Lab/pit mixes, were lying on their beds, still unaware of what was to come.

"Get the dogs out of the house!" he screamed, recalling a recent incident where the mayor of a nearby township had been mistakenly home-invaded by SWAT officers who had shot and killed the family dogs.

Caruso turned back to the front door, saw the lines of red laser beams coming from the muzzles of their rifles. He glanced down at his chest and saw multiple red dots, bouncing there. He raised his hands. The men busted through the front door, a ram tearing the door from its frame. He heard the men yell at him to get down on the ground, and what sounded like an explosion on the lower level (he'd later see that the intruders had destroyed the basement door and its frame as well), and now he dropped to his knees amid their shouted orders and he was pushed to the floor, onto his chest. Someone pulled his arms roughly behind him. Someone cuffed him with plastic zip ties. He saw black boots moving quickly and heard their pounding on hardwood. His sight line was on the family room, where he saw with relief that Angie had gotten the dogs outside (they were barking insanely now, baring their teeth and bumping their snouts against the rear glass door), and then his heart dropped as he saw something that he would never forget: two men standing over his wife and their thirteen-year-old daughter, pointing their rifles at them, their fingers inside the trigger guards, his daughter visibly shaking, her mouth open but unable to speak, paralyzed.

A police officer held his biceps as he lay on the floor.

"Please don't shoot my dogs," Caruso said.

"We're not going to" was the bored reply.

Caruso heard one of the men laugh.

———

A little while later a man cut through the plastic ties binding Caruso's wrists. He got up without assistance, feeling every one of his forty-nine years. His shoulders ached, the result of his arms being forced back. He was wearing gym shorts and an old T-shirt, and though solidly built he was of average height and weight, and he felt small walking by the police, who were bulked up with muscle and further by the added layers of Kevlar.

Caruso arrived at the open area of his house, which consisted of the kitchen, a dining area, and a family room holding a couch, an easy chair, and a large-screen TV. Angie was seated at the kitchen table in a ladder-back chair, Gianna in a chair close beside her. There was a middle-aged man seated at the table as well. He wore a brown suit.

"I'm Detective Brown," said the man, Caruso thinking, *Like the suit.* "Have a seat." A document and other paperwork rested on the kitchen table.

Caruso rubbed at his wrists where the ties had irritated his skin. He took a seat, glanced at Angie. She was outwardly calm and was holding Gianna's hand under the table. Caruso cut his eyes away from her. He couldn't bear to look at either of them.

"Do you know what this is about?" said Brown.

"No, I don't know," said Caruso, hearing the annoyance in his voice. "I assume it has something to do with my oldest son."

"That's correct," said Brown, pushing a document across the table. "Read this."

Caruso looked at the document, addressed to his county's police chief, from a Detective Austin Wilson, signed at the bottom of the page by a district court judge (the last name of the signature was illegible; only the first name, Norman, was readable). Caruso noted the time recorded under the signature: 2:15 a.m. So they'd woken up a judge in the middle of the night to sign a warrant. Caruso wondered if the judge had read it carefully, or had even read it.

In seven pages the document detailed the justification for a search-and-seizure warrant, based on the alleged recent criminal activities of Vincenzo Caruso. Caruso read the document absently, feeling his blood pressure rise as he heard the uniformed invaders go room to room in his house, continuing their search for...what?

"To your knowledge are there any guns in this house?" said Brown, as if he had anticipated Caruso's question.

"I don't own a gun," said Caruso.

"That's not what I asked you."

"To our knowledge, no," said Angie.

Caruso continued to read the warrant. Though he was coming to an understanding of the general nature of his son's offenses, he was distracted by the sounds of the armed men moving about on the second floor.

"You have a good selection of high-shelf liquor in the dining room," said Brown, apropos of nothing. Caruso looked at him, a lightly freckled, light-skinned man, soft in the middle, wearing a mustache he couldn't fully get. His eyes held amusement.

"Why did you say that?" said Caruso.

"You got nice things, is all. That's a real pretty watch you got in your bedroom, too. What is that, a Tag?"

"What the *hell*?"

Angie saw Caruso's eye twitch and she said, "*Joe.*"

Caruso took her implicit advice and held his tongue. Anger would only make things worse. He continued to skim the document. He finished it and said, "My son's not here, obviously. Do you have him in custody?"

"Not as of yet. Do you know where he is?"

"He didn't come home last night."

"He's only eighteen," said Brown. "Is that normal? For him to not come home at night? I'm asking, do you and your wife keep tabs on where he's at—"

"Nothing is normal right this minute," said Angie.

"Well," said Brown, "I suggest you try to contact him. Tell him to surrender himself immediately. It'll be better for him if he does that. You get my drift?"

"What about the damage these people did to my house?" said Caruso.

"That document you just read is what's known as a no-knock warrant. Whatever damage that was done, you're responsible for taking care of it yourself, under the law."

"This is bullshit," said Caruso, quietly.

"You don't have any recourse," said Brown, in a tone that suggested he cared not one ounce. He pointed at the search-and-seizure warrant. "That's your copy."

Brown got up out of his chair without another word. A group of uniformed men came down the stairs to the open area and together with Brown they made their way to the front of the house.

"You okay, Gianna?" said Caruso. "Honey?" It was the first time he had spoken to her. She nodded but didn't answer. Angie was staring at him. He could feel it, but he didn't look her way.

Caruso rose, walked from the open area to the short, narrow hallway that led to the front of the house. There, in the living room where he read his morning paper, stood one of the uniformed police, clad in black and Kevlar, cradling a rifle. He was bodybuilder big, with the kind of size that comes with chemicals and is unattainable with free weights alone. He was in his thirties and had a boot-camp haircut. He was looking at Caruso's books, which took up an entire wall of built-in shelves.

"You got a lot of books," said the police officer. "You must be real smart."

"You guys are done here, right?" said Caruso. "I'd like you to leave my house."

"Sure thing." But he didn't move.

"What's your name?" said Caruso.

"Garrett Lewis," he said, looking Caruso in the eye. "I was told you write articles for magazines. You write a lot of stuff about police."

"That's right."

"Maybe you'll write about this someday."

Garrett Lewis smiled at Caruso and walked out of the house.

Caruso stood at the door and looked out at the scene. One van had already left, and the van that remained was waiting for Lewis. He climbed into the open side door, which then slid shut. Brown was pulling off the curb in his unmarked. Some of the neighbors had gathered on the sidewalk, and one of them was talking to a uniformed county officer who had come out of a patrol car. Caruso and his wife would have to deal with the neighborhood fallout and the chatter on the listserv. He really didn't care.

The door and its frame were destroyed. He assumed the door on the lower level had been violently breached in the same way. They'd have to check out the rest of the house to assess the level of damage the invaders had caused, the cost.

Later, Vince told him that his gold crucifix and chain, inherited from Caruso's father, was missing. Vince had left it on his bedroom dresser when he'd gone out the previous night. So one of the police officers had stolen it.

"You don't have any recourse."

Caruso and Angie spent the remainder of that morning moving about the house quietly, in avoidance of one another. Angie stayed close with Gianna in Gianna's bedroom, talking with their daughter and giving her assurances that "it" was over, that the men with guns would never return to their home.

"Everything's going to be all right, Gianna," said Angie, before the both of them went upstairs, and she shot Caruso a look. "Isn't that right, Joe?"

"Yes, absolutely," said Caruso, trying for but not achieving conviction. He was reminded of a friend, the film critic for the local daily newspaper, who once gave him a concise definition of film noir: "Nothing is going to be all right, ever."

When he was certain he was alone, Caruso sat down to carefully read the search-and-seizure warrant.

The essential, alleged facts were as follows: Vince and an accomplice, a guy named Lorenzo (no last name indicated), had robbed a marijuana dealer at gunpoint. Or rather, Lorenzo had held a gun on the dealer in the stairwell of a nearby apartment building while Vince stood lookout on the ground floor below. They had phoned the dealer to meet them at the apartment house under the ruse that they would purchase a couple of pounds of marijuana from him. Instead, they took the weed without paying for it. The dealer called the police after the robbery and identified both Lorenzo and Vince as his assailants. Caruso knew that this was something that Vince would not have anticipated: the dealer had fingered

Vince and his accomplice to the police. He had violated "the code."

"Stupid," said Caruso, aloud. Meaning, his son.

Caruso took mental note of the fact that there was no mention of his son using or even touching a gun the night of the robbery. In the warrant, Austin Wilson, the detective in charge of the case, stated that Vincenzo Caruso had been observed earlier in the week "brandishing a handgun." It was obvious to Caruso that this detail had been included to induce the judge to sign the warrant, and that it was probably a lie. Vince had many negative, distressing traits, but he was street-smart. He wouldn't have waved a gun around anywhere in the open.

Caruso phoned his friend Gerry Moskowitz, a seasoned criminal defense attorney whose office was over in a neighboring county. They'd been friends since the first grade. Caruso briefed Gerry on the morning's events and read the warrant to him over the phone.

"Have you called Vince yet?" said Gerry.

"No," said Caruso. "I'm too angry, I don't know how to talk to him right now."

"Give me his number and I'll call him. He probably won't answer, but I'll leave a detailed message."

Caruso gave Gerry the number to Vince's cell.

"I'll tell him what's what," said Gerry, a no-bullshit guy. "He needs to turn himself in. The way they've written the thing, it sounds like he could be armed and dangerous. The cops in your part of the county don't fuck around."

"What's he gonna be charged with?"

"Felony armed robbery."

"But…"

"You and Angie need to steel yourselves. In this state, the use of a handgun in the commission of a felony carries a five-year mandatory sentence."

"What the *fuck*, Gerry. I just read the warrant to you. Vince didn't have the gun."

"Doesn't matter. He's looking at five years." Gerry waited out Caruso's silence. "Look, I'm going to try and contact Vince. Hopefully he'll answer his phone and hopefully he'll listen to what I have to say."

"Okay, Gerry."

"Talk to Angie. You two need to communicate. I've seen this kind of thing tear marriages apart."

"She's upstairs trying to get Gianna calmed down. Gerry, they held guns on my wife and thirteen-year-old daughter."

"Be thankful they didn't shoot anyone."

After the call ended, Caruso stayed put, thinking of what had transpired. How did he feel? He always felt the word *violated*, especially when it was used by men, was overwrought and overdramatic. After all, he hadn't been raped. His house had been invaded and police had put guns on him and his family. But what they'd destroyed could be fixed and replaced. His wife and daughter could get over the trauma, with time. Couldn't they?

He was pissed off at Vince for putting all of this in

motion. Scared for him, too. His oldest son was facing five years in prison. It was too much to digest.

First things first. Vince would need to be booked and would probably spend a night or two in a holding facility. The plan would be to bail him out and prepare him for a court date. Gerry Moskowitz was good at what he did. Caruso would put himself in Gerry's hands.

Okay, he was in a tough spot. What would his own father say? *Dark before the dawn*, some bullshit like that.

He wished he could talk to his dad, but his father had passed long ago. Caruso was on his own.

———————

Gerry Moskowitz phoned Caruso in the afternoon and informed him that Vince had turned himself in. Later that day, Moskowitz phoned Caruso again and said that Vince had been booked and transferred to the county jail. It was too late to do anything about the situation now, but Moskowitz would get Vince out the next day.

Vince had one call and he made it to his father late that night.

"Get me out of here, Dad," said Vince. There was a quiver in his voice. He sounded scared. Caruso could hear men laughing, shouting, and cursing in the background.

"I can't do anything until tomorrow."

"Dad, *please*."

"You made your bed," said Caruso.

After the call, Caruso felt bad for being so cold, then

remembered that his son had expressed no remorse for what he'd done. But that did nothing to assuage Caruso's guilt. Vince was still his son. Caruso was supposed to protect him. And protect his family. But the armed men had come into his house and done what they'd done at will. Held guns on his wife and daughter. Destroyed his property. Laughed about it.

"That's a real pretty watch you got in your bedroom, too."

What could he have done? They had the guns and the badges. They had the no-knock warrant. The warrant allowed them to do anything they wanted to do.

"You don't have any recourse."

"Was that Vince?" said Angie. She had just come into Caruso's office on the first floor of the house.

"Yes," said Caruso. "We'll bring him home in the morning."

"How did he sound?"

"Frightened."

"What did Gerry say? What's the plan?"

"I guess we're going to put all of this in Gerry's hands. Have a family meeting. I don't know what the plan is. Not yet."

He was aware of the annoyance in his voice. Also, he wasn't looking at his wife. He was seated in the chair before his laptop, and she put her hand on his shoulder. She felt him tense up and she drew her hand back.

"I'll call Steve tomorrow," said Caruso. "Get him to bring a crew over here and repair the damage." Steve

Alexander was the contractor who'd built their house, seven years earlier.

"I don't care about that," said Angie.

"*I* do," said Caruso.

"You're talking about *things*. We're all still here and we're alive."

Caruso didn't answer. He wasn't in the mood to count his blessings.

"Should we call Paolo and tell him what happened?"

Paolo, sixteen, was their middle child. The "good" son. Another of their kids to whom they'd given a traditional Italian name—somewhat silly, as Caruso was third generation, and about as Italian as pastrami on rye. Paolo was currently on vacation with another family at the beach.

"Let's just tell him when he comes home next week," said Caruso.

"Okay," said Angie.

"I'm sorry," said Caruso.

"For what? You didn't do anything wrong."

I didn't protect us.

Caruso said nothing and the silence in his office was a weight.

"I'm going upstairs and check on Gianna," said Angie. "And then I'm going to bed."

"Go ahead."

"We'll get through this."

"Sure."

"I love you, Joe."

He switched off his lamp and sat in the darkened office, listening to Angie's slow footsteps on the stairs.

———————

Caruso never thought of his son Vince as a bad person. He'd never bullied anyone or fought someone weaker than him, and his parents had never heard him use words like *faggot* and *retard*—words that Caruso himself had used freely in his youth. It's true that Vince was a little bit in love with his self-image as an outlaw type. He had been this way even before he'd hit his teens. He thought of himself as street, and conducted himself in that manner, even though Caruso made a nice living and provided more than any family could need. Every three years, Caruso, with "the book and TV money," bought a new car for Angie (and for himself, if something caught his eye). He also regularly replaced their primary television set for one with a larger screen, for the simple reason that he could.

Vince had a lot of friends. He was popular and athletic. He was strong for his age, and as he reached his teens he got jacked. His father had taught him the rudiments of boxing (weight on the back foot, elbows tucked in, pivot your hip into the punch) but Vince figured out correctly, at a young age, that technique was secondary to will and confidence, and that many fights were won before the first punch was thrown. He wasn't afraid of anyone. He liked to fight.

He was a white kid who hung with Black kids. He had white friends but not many. He had come up playing peewee football and the team in his neighborhood mostly consisted of Black players. The white parents in his area generally didn't allow their sons to play tackle football. Some objected to the violent nature of the sport; they didn't want their sons to get hurt, or to hurt anyone. Vince's father encouraged him to play. His mother, if she was not exactly happy about it, didn't object. Because Vince could hit and take a hit, he gained the respect of the Black boys who were on the team, and their friendship. Most of his teammates had earned nicknames. Vince's was "Mountain Man." It was because he was white. Didn't make much sense, as Vince was not a country type, but it stuck.

He entered public high school and played for the team at defensive end and was good. Not college-level good, but a starter. He had also been smoking weed, going back to the sixth grade. Most all of the kids he hung with got high. Some got their heads up recreationally, and some fell in love with it. He was in the latter group. He was straight on game days, but otherwise stayed high. His schoolwork suffered, and anyway it was not a priority.

By senior year he didn't care about football either and the coach lost interest in him and benched him. His teachers gave up on him as well, partly because of his attitude. Vince was not on track to go to college. He got suspended a couple of times for behavior issues. Joe and Angie met with the principal, a woman named Leslie

Harrison ("Dr." Leslie Harrison, and she asked to be addressed as such), who seemed uninterested in Vince's situation. Caruso got the vibe ten minutes into the conversation, and in a way he understood her indifference. Vince was going to graduate soon (barely fulfilling the requirements) and be gone, which was a relief to her. There was nothing she could do to help or change him at this point, and a principal was judged (and promoted) by his or her success stories. At least for this woman, the failures were better off forgotten.

Vince graduated in June and turned eighteen in July. In August, he was arrested and charged as an adult with Felony Armed Robbery.

———————

Joe Caruso officially hired Gerry Moskowitz to represent Vince at his trial. Gerry was good in court and was known by most of the judges in the county. Gerry was practically part of the Caruso family, he had been there for Vince's birthday parties and was familiar with his history. Caruso had unloaded to Gerry over the years, over beers and shots, about his eldest son.

The first meeting, in Gerry's office, with Vince, Caruso, and Angie in attendance, did not go well. Vince was cocky despite the serious nature of the charges, and Caruso lost his patience with him quickly. They had barely been talking at home since Vince's arrest. Gerry told Vince that in advance of his court date he would need to get a full-time job, buy a blue suit, and grow his hair out a little. (Vince got his shape-up at a barbershop on Georgia Avenue where his Black friends went, and kept his hair down to the scalp with a slash cut for a part; Gerry was telling him, implicitly, that he "looked like" a tough young Black guy—not a positive for court.) Vince didn't like the last suggestion, and Caruso told him to "shut the fuck up and listen to Mr. Moskowitz, he's trying to help."

Caruso asked a Greek friend, Costas Colouris, who owned CC's, a heating and cooling business, if he could put Vince on as a helper, and Costas agreed. It was a good situation for all. So now Vince was out of the house early in the morning and most of the day, which allowed Caruso to work without stress (the mood in their home had become very tense). And Vince didn't mind working that kind of job. In fact it suited him. Unlike his father, he was handy, so he quickly took to the mechanics of installing and repairing air conditioners and furnaces. As for Costas, a tough guy whose own soft sons had shown no interest in the business, he liked Vince and enjoyed his company.

The fraught atmosphere at home was not only between Caruso and Vince. Gianna had become withdrawn and very quiet since the police had invaded their home. She had trouble sleeping and when she did, she said, her dreams were upsetting. Angie had Gianna talk to a psychiatrist who was on staff at the "woman's practice" (internal medicine and gynecology) where the two of them shared a doctor. Gianna did not want to speak about the police raid, which told the psychiatrist that it had impacted her deeply. "They had guns pointed at her face," said Angie, and the shrink said, "Your daughter is suffering from a form of PTSD." She suggested antidepressants but Angie was hesitant to give drugs to a girl of thirteen.

Their son Paolo skated above it all. He was the kid who always did his homework without being told to, who wanted to get good grades, not for his parents, but for himself. Of course, he had not been there "that day," so he was unscathed. Caruso and Angie didn't worry about Paolo; he had always been self-sufficient (if a bit remote). He'd be fine.

Caruso and Angie's relationship had cooled after the home invasion. They spoke as often as they always had but Angie avoided discussion about Vince's situation because it got a negative reaction from her husband. Like many couples who had been married for twenty-plus years, they had settled on an informal schedule of lovemaking once a week or so, but now it was with less frequency, sometimes once a month. Neither of them, when thinking about it to themselves, could explain why. The desire was simply not at the forefront, there were too many other elements pushing it off the menu. There wasn't room for it in their lives.

Angie told herself that the tension would be relieved soon, that it was natural to be on edge: Their son was looking at five years in federal prison. Waiting for the trial, which had been postponed several times, was agonizing.

Caruso planned to write about no-knock warrants as his next project. He told Angie that it would serve as his therapy. He felt there was a book "in it" and had sold his lit agent on the idea. It was after all in his wheelhouse. Investigations of police tactics and systemic corruption is what he did.

He had started out writing for the local alternative weekly, penning stories about city and county crime. He covered the trials of drug dealers and hitters during the high crime years, when those people were household names. There wasn't any money in it and making their nut was a struggle for him and Angie, who worked in production design for a business magazine and was also underpaid. Caruso started writing features for Sunday newspaper magazines, which was more lucrative but not much. Then a comprehensive piece he wrote for the *Los Angeles Times Magazine* on the Rampart CRASH unit and the attendant scandal changed his life. He next published a book on the subject, *First District*, which got optioned for television. As part of the deal, Caruso's savvy agent tied him as screenwriter to the pilot, a service to be included in the option money. The production company accepted this arrangement, as it was costing them nothing, but insisted that he be paired with an experienced television writer. Caruso, it turned out, had no aptitude for screenwriting (like many journalists and nonfiction writers, he was not a natural dramatist), but he got the co-credit on the pilot, which went to series. The series was a hit and ran for five seasons. Because he had cowritten the pilot, Caruso got a piece of the action on all subsequent episodes.

His next nonfiction book, a look at the day-to-day workings of a police station in D.C.'s First District, likewise sold to television. It became a network show called *District One* (though no one on the force had ever used that term, it was deemed a catchier title). Some of the storylines involved "bad cops," but at the end of the hour they were found out and ostracized by all the good ones, and the world, for the viewer, was set right again. Wish-fulfillment entertainment: cases closed, problems solved.

District One was a success. When it went to syndication, as popular episodic television often does, he began to get substantial residual checks in the mail with regularity. Caruso and his family were suddenly wealthy.

But now he was locked into a formula. He had other interests, but he couldn't afford to explore them. He was known for writing books about police and police corruption. It had earned him a great deal of money. The handcuffs were made of gold.

The court date arrived, almost a year to the day after Vince's arrest. They drove that morning in a very quiet car to the district courthouse. Vince was to plead guilty, so it was a nonjury sentencing trial. Caruso, Angie, and Vince dressed appropriately. Vince in his blue suit looked like a young professional. Angie liked him with his hair grown out, it reminded her of how he looked when he was a boy.

Vince was contrite in front of the judge, a middle-aged Black man whose name was familiar to Caruso from stories in the local newspaper. The judge and Gerry Moskowitz exchanged pleasantries at the outset, it was obvious that they knew each other. Then the plea was officially entered. Vince offered his sincere apologies for committing the crime in question, talked about his life since his arrest, his job, and his commitment to keeping himself centered and straight. Afterward, Caruso stood and spoke on behalf of his son. What he said had been carefully written and rehearsed, but it was from the heart. A young male lawyer in the gallery was smiling at Caruso as he spoke, as if something was funny. Caruso's blood jumped, he wanted to slap the smile off that cunt's face, but he got through the speech, which was really a plea for mercy.

The judge drew his decision out, which only heightened the tension. Then he sentenced Vince to five years' probation. Angie and Caruso visibly decompressed, they turned to each other and hugged. Their son was not going to prison.

In his closing comments the judge addressed Caruso, mentioning that he was a fan of *District One*. Caruso was privately embarrassed to be associated with the show. It was nothing like his book, which examined all aspects of a police station—the day-to-day lives of the officers and the brass, their successes and failures. In the series pilot, the Commander of the First District walks into a hostage situation with her service weapon drawn and takes down the perpetrator with a head shot (which would never happen).

She investigates a white-collar conspiracy herself, exposing a wealthy real estate developer for his crimes (which would never happen). A dirty cop is exposed, thereby "solving" police corruption in the First District (ignoring systemic issues that enable corruption). The usual bullshit of network television. So, yeah, Caruso didn't care for the show, but he cashed the checks.

Caruso thanked the judge. He meant it. He'd never forget the judge's reasoning, and his kindness.

That afternoon, they cut a cake at the house. Gerry followed them there in his Mercedes sedan. Paolo and Gianna joined in, though they were not in particularly celebratory moods. Paolo looked up to Vince for his toughness, and he was glad he was not going to do time, but that kind of hero worship, common in kid brothers, had begun to wane. Paolo already had his eye on an out-of-state college and was looking forward to leaving home. Gianna hugged Vince, she was happy for him, happy for the family. But she held some bitterness for Vince and for what he had brought into the house. She mostly stayed in her room these days. She didn't like being out in the world anymore. There were people on the street with guns. She grew agitated and frightened at the sight of police.

Caruso asked Gerry if he wanted something "more" than a beer. Gerry said it was too early for that.

"Vincenzo," said Caruso. "You want a drink?"

"No, Dad," said Vince. "Thanks." Vince had never liked alcohol.

"I'm going to have one," said Caruso. "It's a great day."

He had the money to drink the good stuff. He liked bourbon. He poured himself a Blanton's, three fingers, neat.

———————

It had not escaped Angie that Caruso had been drinking more, and steadily, since Vince's arrest. It was mildly troubling, but she didn't bother him about it, didn't want to pile on while he was under the pressure of Vince's impending sentencing. If the news was good for Vince, she thought, Caruso would cut back.

Caruso had enjoyed a glass or two of red in the past, one with dinner and maybe one later in the night, but then he started in on the liquor, a little bourbon while he read and listened to music in the living room after the sun went down.

"Just a taste," he'd say.

He posited it as a new hobby. People were into this bourbon thing, the way they had been into cigars a few years ago. He spoke about "tastings." He only drank what he called "high shelf," but not top shelf, and not too expensive, because he was going through it pretty quickly. He liked Old Forester 1920, Elijah Craig and Four Roses (small batch for both), Sagamore Rye (not bourbon but tasty), and his favorite, Blanton's—that is, when he could get it. "It's sipping whiskey," he said to Angie. He liked Wild Turkey 101 too, not considered "sipping whiskey" but, man, the high proof got him there fast. One or two every night these days (okay, *always* two), and later some wine on top of it, which fogged him nicely. "Never mix the grain with the grape," he'd told Angie in the past, now forgetting his own clichéd words of wisdom.

He felt good at night, the alcohol was a distraction (meaning it made him forget), but it fucked up his mornings. Angie noticed he wasn't getting much writing done. Sure, he was in his office at 9, like always, seated in front of his laptop. He spent a lot of time on the internet ("I'm doing my research"), but nothing was getting typed onto the screen.

After Vince got probation, Angie figured her husband would slow down. He didn't. Caruso still did something physical every day (long walks, bike rides a couple of times a week, push-ups and dumbbell work in the basement), but he began to get a paunch and there were new lines on his face. The alcohol was working him.

It was true, what Angie had heard, that the hands on a clock spin quickly for the middle-aged. She had long ago left her job at the magazine. To fill her days she volunteered for a church-based nonprofit that delivered food to people who, for one reason or another (age, infirmity, mental illness), could or would no longer leave their homes. She made friends easily and sometimes went out for lunch with her co-workers. She and the chef (longish hair, tats) who worked in the basement of the church had developed a mutual attraction. He was younger than Angie and she was flattered, but no. Admittedly her marriage with Caruso had no physical component to it now but adultery was not on her docket. Still, it was nice to think about it. She looked forward to going to work.

Paolo finished college (Colorado State in Boulder) and shortly thereafter got an entry-level position on Wall Street.

Gianna was about to graduate from the local public high school. She was darkly attractive in the Mediterranean fashion of her mother, had a small circle of friends, and was very particular about her choice of young men. She flirted occasionally but didn't date. Gianna had trust issues with males. She wasn't involved in extracurricular activities at school, which put her at a disadvantage when applying to colleges, but her grades were well above average and she managed to get accepted to a state school about an hour away from home. She was headed there in the fall.

Vince had charmed his probation officer, a woman named Yolanda, as he had charmed many people since childhood. So the years after his conviction had not been stressful for him, as Yolanda kept him on a very loose leash, and he saw her less and less. She liked him, and also he had kept his commitment to staying employed and staying out of trouble with the law. Eventually his father rehired Gerry Markowitz and they went before another county judge and managed to get Vince's felony conviction expunged. This broadened Vince's opportunities.

Vince took classes and got into the local steamfitters union. He reluctantly left Costas Colouris, as they had a nice relationship, for a gig in the physical plant of an apartment complex, and later applied for a position servicing and installing heating and cooling systems for a major government defense contractor. This required a security clearance. As he was no longer a felon, he qualified and got the job.

Caruso still had a contract for his book but had not gone past the research phase. His lit agent was losing his patience, but Caruso ignored the static. He spent time in libraries but got distracted by other subject matter while there. He talked to cops who had been his sources for the *First District* book. He flew to the Midwest to interview the family of an innocent woman killed in a no-knock raid, and returned with what he said was "great stuff, great ammunition," but he never did get it down on paper. For balance he interviewed the wife of a police officer killed during a similar raid (in addition to civilian deaths, there were a surprising number of police fatalities in no-knock shoot-outs).

"It's there," Caruso told Angie. "I just can't figure out a way in. I'm staring at a blank screen. I'm not blocked, Angie—it's not like I'm trying to write a novel or sumshit and I can't find a way to enter a fictional world. I have the facts. It's like, I don't know, it's like I've forgotten how to write."

"Maybe you're too close to it," said Angie, gently. It was at night, they were seated at the kitchen table, and as usual Caruso had been drinking. "It's hard for you to be objective on the subject."

"Yeah, it's fucking hard. I *am* close to it. I built this house, and those SWAT guys destroyed it. They did thousands of dollars in damage, and they stole Vince's cross and laughed about it. They put guns on you and my little girl. For what? To arrest a guy who they knew was not a violent offender. It said right in the warrant that he didn't have a gun the night they robbed that marijuana dealer."

"It also said in the warrant that Vince was brandishing a gun earlier in the day."

"Which was bullshit," said Caruso. "A lie. That was put in there to persuade that judge to sign the warrant in the middle of the night."

"You don't know that it was a lie," said Angie.

He *didn't* know. But he'd convinced himself that it was true.

In 2018, Caruso went to a luncheon where he was to receive an award, with several others, for local influencers who had "made a difference" in the area. One of the awardees was the former police chief, recently retired, of their county. Caruso nodded at him by way of recognition and in return he got a stony, hard look. It wasn't his imagination. The guy was eye-fucking him.

That night, after a couple of bourbons and a glass of wine, he unloaded on Angie.

"Why do you think that police chief had a hard-on for me?" said Caruso.

"I don't know," said Angie. She had been there at the luncheon but she hadn't noticed anything.

"You know how things were under him in the county? Why would they give *him* an award? I've been out to the jail, up-county, to give talks to the inmates. You know what you see out there? Young Black and Brown men and women in jumpsuits. Hardly any white kids, ever. Most of them are repeat nonviolent drug offenders."

"What are you saying?"

"It's a proven fact that white kids use and sell marijuana at the same rate as Black and Brown kids, but in our county white kids rarely get busted for it. They sure as shit don't do time for it. On any given night you can drive around here in the east part of the county and see Black kids sitting on the curb with three or four squad cars surrounding their vehicle. Go to the west side, you *never* see that. Shit, they got undercover cops hiding in our park, waiting for the kids to get out of school so they can bust them for smoking weed. They don't do that in the parks on the west side of the county."

"I know. We've spoken about this. But you've never written about it. So why do you think that guy was angry at you?"

"His name was on the letterhead of the no-knock warrant request. I guess he just doesn't like me."

"Joe…"

"That fucking SWAT guy, Garrett Lewis, I'll never

forget his name, he said, 'Maybe you'll write about this someday,' before he left our house. They all knew who I was. To them I'm the fucking asshole who writes about corrupt police. Honey, that's why they targeted our family."

"I don't believe that."

"I do. I'm *starting* to…"

"Joseph, you're…"

"Paranoid?"

"I didn't say that." But *paranoid* was exactly the word that was in her head.

"They stole my son's cross," said Caruso, quietly. "My father gave Vince that cross for his baptism."

Angie put her hand over Caruso's to comfort him. His eyes were bloodshot. He didn't look like the man she'd married.

———————

Vince drove his work truck over to his parents' house and parked on the street. He had an apartment nearby now, but visited his folks several times a week.

Vince took the steps up to the front porch where he had played when he was a child. The Caruso house was atop a rise, facing south, so late in the day the porch caught the full blast of the setting sun in the west. The sun was bright and warm on him now. Vince's mother called it "golden time," and in his childhood it had been Vince's favorite time of day.

Vince used his key to enter. His mother was in the kitchen at the back of the house, making salsa from the tomatoes and peppers she had harvested from her garden.

"Vinny," said Angie.

"Hey, Mom."

She kissed him on his cheek. He took a corn chip from a brown bag and dipped the chip into the salsa, tasted it. She studied him, his healthy coloring, his good build. Waited for his reaction.

"Righteous," he said.

"It'll be better after it sits."

From the kitchen, through the bank of windows framing a screened-in porch, they could see Caruso, working on one of two rosebushes he had planted against the fence after his mother and father died, two years apart. The rosebushes "came back" every year and had grown considerably and were in full bloom.

"I'm gonna go say hi to Dad."

"Okay, honey."

Vince exited through the screen porch and approached his father in the backyard. The lawn was immaculate. His father paid a crew to take care of the yard once a week. Vince remembered when he was kid, when he'd tried to mow the lawn with their old Toro, leaving his father unsatisfied with the results.

As Vince neared him, Caruso reached into a rosebush and pulled on a leafy vine.

"Vincenzo," said Caruso.

"Pop. What's the plan there?"

"Clearing out these vines. You gotta stay on top of it."

"Isn't that what they call an exercise in futility?"

"If you leave them alone, the vines win."

Vince could see small drops of blood on one of Caruso's hands, where he had caught a thorn.

"Don't you pay guys to do that?" said Vince.

"This isn't in their contract." Caruso pulled the vine free and tossed it aside. Looked at his son straight on. "You just getting off?"

"Yeah."

"How's work?"

"Good."

"Making sure all those defense contractors are cool and comfy?"

"Doing my part for democracy. How about you? Working on anything?"

Caruso shook his head. "Seems like I'm retired."

"You're too young for that."

"Don't worry, there's plenty of money. You'll be all right."

"I'm all right *now*," said Vince.

He knew his father was kidding, but Vince didn't care for the joke. It wasn't the first time his father had implied that his own success would equal a sizable inheritance for his kids. Vince resented the notion that he needed a windfall, or wanted one.

"I know you're all right," said Caruso. "You're doing great."

He mostly meant it. Vince was gainfully employed,

a skilled worker, and, still in his twenties, was making upward of seventy K a year. The union gave him health insurance and a pension. He was a productive member of society. That's what Joe Caruso had told his friends that he wanted out of his kids, nothing more. Still, this was Vince, with all of his potential. Who knows how far he could have gone, if he hadn't fucked up and committed a felony…

"You mean, great for *me*," said Vince.

"I didn't say that."

"You know, Dad, I…I wish I hadn't done what I did."

"I know it."

"There's not a day goes by that I don't think about what I brought down on you and Mom, and Gianna. I gotta live with that forever. But that was ten years ago, right? I did my probation and I stayed out of trouble. I learned a trade and worked hard. I've managed to get past it, mostly. I wish you could, too."

"I have," said Caruso, waving his hand. "It's forgotten. It's nothing."

They both knew that was a lie, but Vince said nothing more.

"Come here," said Caruso, and Vince stepped into his arms. Caruso hugged him, squeezed him tightly. Vince stepped back, nodded. His father looked old and blown.

Vince stayed for dinner. Afterward, he stepped out on the screen porch and lit a joint.

From the kitchen table, where Caruso and Angie still sat, they watched him.

"He's still smoking that shit," sad Caruso.

"He doesn't drink," said Angie, and Caruso gave her a look. "Leave him alone."

Caruso sat back, his eyes watery. He touched the stem of the wineglass before him. Angie stood and began to clear the dishes from the table.

———————

One night, Caruso had been drinking bourbon alone in the living room, sitting in his chair by the fire, not reading or even listening to music, brooding, his mood darkening with each sip. Angie came into the room and took a seat on the couch, close to him.

"It's quiet in here," said Angie.

"I'm good with that."

"You want to talk?"

"Sure," said Caruso.

But then there was a long silence. A bronze Ansonia clock that had belonged to his grandparents, set on the fireplace mantel, ticked loudly.

"I was thinking about Vince," said Caruso.

"What about him?"

"When he was a kid, he wasn't even in school yet, he was about four, I guess. I used to strap him into that seat I had, in the rack thing I had mounted over the rear wheel of my bike. It was that Trek I used to own. The seat was made of plastic. It was low-tech, probably not even entirely safe. Anyway, I'd put a helmet on him and we'd ride that path in the park. Not a casual ride, either, I'd go fast. I could hear him laughing back there, and when I'd turn my head, he'd have his little arms spread out, like he was flying. I wonder if he even remembers."

"He's mentioned it. He remembers some of it. The sensations."

"And then, in those same years, at the playground, when he'd do things on the jungle-gym bars that none of the other boys his age could do, or were brave enough to do. He was fearless. The other fathers who were there, I felt like they were envious, like. Everyone thought the kid was really special."

"He was. He *is*."

Caruso took a drink and set the glass down on the table beside him. "Up until that day they raided our house, I felt like I had done a good job. That everything was all right, you know? That I'd done a good job as a father. But it wasn't all right. Vince had gone off the rails. I was so busy with my career and everything, I missed it. How could I miss it, Ange?"

"I guess we were both kind of unaware. But so what? Our family is okay. We got through everything and here we are."

"*Where* are we?" said Caruso. The desperation in his voice frightened her.

"Tell me what's wrong," she said.

"I don't know. I used to wake up in the morning and my eyes would snap open. I knew I had work to do and I couldn't wait to strap on my shoes and go *to* it. I wake up now, I don't even feel the need to get out of bed. For what? There's nothing to look forward to, Angie. Nothing."

"Joe," said Angie. "You should talk to someone."

"A shrink? That's for weaklings."

"No, it isn't. You know better than that."

"A shrink is going to *fix* things? Angie, I failed."

"Joseph…"

"Everything's fucked."

She reached for his hand and held it. He didn't look her way.

———

A couple of years later, Vince, who had dated mostly Black women since his youth, came by the house with his girlfriend, a woman named Martina. Martina was dark-skinned and a first-generation American of Jamaican descent. She was attractive, lively, a hard charger in the mortgage-refinance business, and in love. Angie could see that Vince was, too. They were living together in Vince's apartment. He was looking for a bigger place. It was plain to Angie where this was going, and she was pleased.

Vince at thirty-two was in excellent physical shape, though his hairline had begun to recede and there were flecks of gray in his beard. He still got his shape-up at the Black barbershop up the street and had kept the friend-ships of his youth. Some in his crowd were professionals, some married with families, others were trying, a few had done time, and a couple of them had passed, one violently.

It is a strange sensation, thought Angie, to see your child begin to grow old, but it was not upsetting. How could something so natural be distressing? She looked forward to grandchildren and the changing seasons. Considering everything, she felt fortunate.

Paolo had dated many women, some who liked him, and some who liked him for his money, and was currently without a steady partner. Angie was confident he'd find someone. Paolo was a venture capitalist, financially successful, and still living in Manhattan. His condo was high in a building in the mid-Fifties and gave to a view of the East River. Angie couldn't fathom a ten-thousand-dollar-a-month mortgage payment but kept her reservations to herself. After years of emotional separation, Paolo and Vince had become close again and were spending time together. Vince often made the trip up north as Paolo did not like to leave New York.

Gianna was a nurse at a local hospital and was taking classes, hoping to become a physician's assistant. She had found someone after years of defective relationships with men who Angie felt, naturally, were unworthy of her. Angie liked this one, a Black man in his late thirties who was the manager of a restaurant now and planned to have his own eatery someday. It seemed that, between Vince and Gianna, Angie's extended family was going to be multiracial. What was rare in Angie's youth had become commonplace today, at least in the area where they lived. In any event, Gianna was settled, though she was on medication to fight depression and occasionally saw a psychiatrist. She had never entirely put the raid on their home behind her, but she would be fine.

Angie was thinking of this when she called Gerry Moskowitz and asked him about the judge who had signed the warrant for the no-knock raid on their house. She had a first name, per the document in her files, but the last name of his signature was unreadable.

"Why do you want to know?" said Gerry.

"I'm curious, is all. His first name was Norman."

"I'll get back to you," said Gerry.

Gerry called her a few days later. He was busy, and getting the information to her was not a priority for him. Plus, he had been hesitant to give her the name, until he discovered the judge's fate.

"The judge was Norman Ludwig," said Gerry. "I had some dealings with him. Not a bad guy."

"Is he still on the bench?"

"He's dead. Died a few years ago, from what I understand."

"What did he die of?"

"No idea. Would you be happy if I told you it was a slow and painful death?"

"Not at all. You know me better than that."

"The no-knock wasn't his fault, Angie. It's a fault of the system."

"Yeah, I've heard that. Gerry?"

"What?"

"What's this phone call gonna cost me? Six, seven hundred dollars?"

"It's eight hundred for a phone call now."

"Why, because you need a new Benz?"

"Need's got nothing to do with it."

"See you around, Gerry. Thank you."

Thinking of the judge put Angie on a mental jag that took her into the neighborhood of Unfinished Business. She was sixty-one now, and some of her friends had begun to pass. It would be satisfying to have some answers before death knocked on her own door. She was not obsessed whatsoever with the raid on their house, in fact she had made peace with it long ago, but still there were things she'd like to know.

In her husband's office she powered up his laptop. There on the home screen was an icon for a program that found the current address and contact information for people, commonly used by private detectives and security types. Caruso had put the payment for the program on an active credit card. The program's annual fee was paid automatically, so it was still operative. She quickly found what she was looking for.

Caruso had spoken of Garrett Lewis many times after the raid. He was the big SWAT guy, "jacked up on steroids," who had said something snide to Caruso before leaving their house. Lewis obviously knew that Caruso wrote magazine articles and nonfiction books about police corruption, and Lewis had been mocking him.

Angie's intention was to talk with Lewis and find out why. There was something else she wanted to ask him, too.

She found his house, a rambler, in a neighborhood of modest single-family homes with streets named after World War II generals. A Z71 Suburban, the largest and most powerful Chevy SUV available, was parked in Lewis's driveway. His choice of vehicles did not surprise her, and neither did the pair of fake testicles hanging from the tow hitch. Angie parked on his street and waited. After an hour or so, no one emerged from the house, and she decided to go home.

Angie returned the next day, parked in roughly the same spot, and watched Lewis's house. She took photos of his residence with her iPhone, because she could. Somewhere in the back of her mind she knew that what she was doing was irrational, but then the police had done the same to her family's home. Her husband had remembered seeing a black SUV with heavily tinted windows pull up in front of their house a couple of days before the raid. Whoever was in the SUV took several photos of the house (Caruso had seen the flashes go off). It seemed odd to him at the time, until after the raid when he realized that his family had been surveilled. Now Angie was doing the same thing. She didn't quite know why.

She had been there for a couple of hours when Garrett Lewis came out of the house and walked to his SUV. He was a big man but nowhere near as massive as Caruso had described. His head was shaved and he had a paunch. There were no items in the yard or on the porch to indicate children. There was no other vehicle in front of the house. Angie guessed that he was single, either never married or divorced.

He drove off and she followed him, staying far back. Then, on the main road, she kept herself behind other cars. Anyone who watched cop shows knew how to execute a tail. There was no danger in him dusting her. His vehicle was so large, it was hard to lose sight of it.

He pulled into a freestanding local pub that had been in business for forty-some years. It was frequented by adults who had not moved far, geographically or emotionally, from their high schools. It had evolved from an Olde English deal into a sports bar but was mainly just a place to drink draft beer and see familiar faces. Garrett Lewis parked his Suburban and went inside. Angie waited in the lot for about fifteen minutes, gathered herself, and said out loud, "Why not?"

She found him at the bar, seated on a stool by himself. He had a mug of draft before him and he was looking at a television screen on the wall where two men argued about something to do with the NFL in an artificially heated manner. Angie took a seat beside him.

He looked at her briefly, then looked away. Seeing a woman ten years older than him was enough to make him lose interest, but he gave her a courtesy nod. She said, "Hi," and he chucked up his chin politely and returned his gaze to the screen.

She sized him up. He'd gone soft in the middle. He had the look of a football player who had stopped working out, and if he had been on steroids at one time, as Caruso had suggested, he was not using them now. His chin had doubled and there were folds on the back of his bald head.

Angie ordered a mug of Budweiser from the bartender. After it was served she said to him, "Are you Garrett Lewis?"

He turned to her warily. "Yeah? Do we know each other?"

"You probably don't remember me. You were on a SWAT team here in the county, right?"

"That's right. Why would I remember you?"

"You and your guys executed a no-knock warrant on my house, thirteen years ago. You were looking to arrest my son, Vince Caruso. It would have said Vincenzo Caruso on the warrant. My name is Angela Caruso, I'm Vince's mother."

"Look, lady…"

"Don't worry. I don't want anything and I'm not crazy."

"Well, it does seem a little crazy to me that you would just show up here after thirteen years. You followed me, right? You must want *something*."

"I only want to talk."

Lewis looked around the bar, as if searching for help. That she was a woman worked in her favor. He thought of himself as a gentleman. If she were a man he probably would've told her to get lost or fuck off.

"Make it brief."

"Do you remember us?" said Angie.

"No," said Lewis, after deliberating whether he should engage her or not. "That was a long time ago. I haven't been with the police for six years."

"My son Vince was involved in an armed robbery. He and an accomplice robbed a marijuana dealer. The accomplice had a gun, not Vince, but Vince was just as guilty in the eyes of the law. He committed a crime."

"Okay..."

"I'm just putting that out there, straightaway. So you don't think I'm in denial of what he did or anything like that."

"Got it."

"You and your squad, or whatever it's called, they came and raided our house."

"Understood. What's your point?"

"I don't know," said Angie, with honesty, letting herself cool down. "I guess I'm just wondering, *why*."

Both of them sipped their beers.

"I was doing my job," he said, quietly.

"I'm trying to understand—"

"I was military first. Army. Did a tour in Iraq, early in the war. And then when I came back, I was like a lot of guys who had done combat duty, I was, like, I don't know. In the service I woke up every day and I got my orders. I had a purpose, OK? There was no equivalent for that feeling in civilian life, so I became a police officer. With my background, wasn't long before I was put on the SWAT team. I mean, going house to house over there, that's what we did, same thing. We had a mission. I didn't need much of a learning curve. I was good at it. Is that what you wanted? The reason for why I landed in that line of work?"

Lewis drank off the rest of his beer and signaled the bartender.

"You didn't think about the damage you did, to property, to families?"

"No. We were apprehending criminals. Like you said, your son committed a crime."

Lewis was not the type for self-reflection. She didn't know why she thought he would be.

"There was a guy in plain clothes that day," said Angie, "a Detective Brown. He was baiting my husband, talking about the expensive watch he saw in our bedroom, stuff like that."

Lewis chuckled. "Brown, yeah...The Black guys in the squad used to call him Detective Beige. Fucking useless, pardon my French. Suits like him were required to come along."

"You said something to my husband, too. You said, 'Maybe you'll write about this someday.' So you knew my husband wrote magazine pieces and books about the police..."

"Well, they brief us before we go in, tell us who the target is, all that. So they probably mentioned who your husband was that morning. You know, I admit, I was kind of cocky back then. And the adrenaline, after a raid, the relief...you say stuff. I didn't mean anything, I was probably just joking around." Lewis nodded his head as it came to him. "I do remember your husband now."

"Joseph Caruso."

"Yeah. My sympathies. I read about him in the papers. It was about a year ago, wasn't it?"

Angie didn't reply.

"I had an uncle," said Lewis, "same kinda deal. None of us expected it. Depression's a bitch."

Angie said nothing. It unsettled Lewis.

"I think we've talked enough," he said. "I've been more than courteous to you."

"I'm leaving," said Angie. "But I have one more question, only one."

"Go ahead."

"One of your guys stole a crucifix from our house that day. My husband's father gave it to my son for his baptism, and it was very special to us. I'm wondering if you know anything about that."

"No, I don't," said Lewis, with authority. "I never took anything as a police officer, not ever. I was straight."

Angie believed him. She stood, reached into her purse and found her wallet.

"Let me get that," said Lewis.

"I'd rather pay for my own," said Angie.

That was the last thing she said to him before she left the bar. She was disappointed. Garrett Lewis barely remembered that day. He was just doing his job. He wasn't a bad guy. Just a cog in a rotten wheel.

———————

Angie was on her laptop, looking at news stories, when she came across a series of articles and podcasts about no-knock warrants in the online version of the *Washington Post*. Written by Courtney Kan, Nicole Dungca, and Jenn Abelson, the series was a thoroughly researched and comprehensive look at the subject, both balanced and damning, that made a good case for banning the practice. It was the kind of piece that Joe Caruso had wanted to write but could never crack. He had been too close to the subject, too obsessed with it, and it had frozen him and clouded his mind.

In recent years, there had been numerous deaths in no-knock raids, both the shooting deaths of citizens and the violent deaths of police officers. There was, most infamously, the case of Breonna Taylor, a Louisville nurse who was fatally shot six times by police who had entered her apartment with the intention of arresting her boyfriend, an alleged drug dealer. There were other killings of people who had not committed crimes, cases of fatalities where the police entered the wrong residence, and cases where low-level dealers were found with minuscule amounts of product in their possession after their deaths at the hands of police.

What was clear from the series was that no-knock warrants and raids were inefficient and often deadly. They didn't work.

———————————

Angie was thinking of putting the house up for sale. Sometimes their home reminded her of the raid and what had happened to them afterward, but that was not her reason for wanting to move. She more often thought about her children when they were little, the laughter inside these walls, the holidays, her relationship with Joe, the life they'd built here, together. It was just that the house was too large for her now. She had no destination in mind yet, but she knew it wouldn't be far from her children.

KNICKERBOCKER

MEMORIES ARE UNRELIABLE, *and so are history books, but truth can be found in both.* Leah Brown was considering this as she drove onto the grounds of New Morning, a residential retirement and nursing-home complex set on the edge of a tributary of Rock Creek Park in Northwest D.C.

She steered her Plymouth Horizon into a visitor's space, killed the engine, and grabbed her book bag off the passenger seat, pushing aside a paperback copy of *Them* by Joyce Carol Oates. It had become a template for the kind of fiction she was hoping to write, and Leah was reading it for the second time. The book was not historical fiction per se, but it put the reader firmly into a specific time and place. That it was a phenomenally mature novel for a debut was inspiring to her. Maybe her ambitions were not a pipe dream or out of reach. She was shooting high, perhaps unrealistically, but better to emulate a genuine talent than a hack.

Leah entered the lobby of the apartment building. She stood out among the geriatric residents, with her late 1970s female rocker–inspired looks, her heavy black eyeliner and black-shag cut, part Joan, part Chrissie. She was a bit old for that, and too old to be wearing her jean jacket adorned with the buttons of her favorite bands, but that was who she was at the time, a slow starter and a bit behind. She was also making a statement. The look was her badge.

She signed in at the desk and went down a first-floor hall, where she knocked on a door. An elderly female voice instructed Leah to enter.

Leah's grandmother, Maria Brown, was seated by the bed in her chair. An afghan blanket, the product of her own handiwork, covered her legs. Maria had knitted colorful afghans for all of her grandchildren, knowing that the blankets they slept under in the winter would be what they remembered of her after she was gone.

"Yiayia," said Leah.

"Come," said Maria, with a gesture of her hand.

Leah pulled a chair over from the breakfast table. Maria's place was called an apartment but it was closer to an efficiency. There was a bedroom, but it was very small, and Maria had decided early on that the living room would be the place where she would sleep. Attendants looked in on her during the day and a nurse, who bathed her and saw to her other needs, spent the night.

Maria's son John, Leah's father, paid for all of this. He was an optometrist with a busy practice. He visited his mother on Sundays.

"Help yourself if you'd like something to drink," said Maria. She spoke clearly, without a quiver in her voice. She was eighty-one and her face was relatively unlined. She had nice skin, free of age spots, with the olive tint of the Greeks. Her cheekbones were defined, her eyes hazel, and her hair, worn long and braided by her nurse, was silver white.

"I'm okay." Leah pulled a notebook and pen from her book bag, along with an Olympic microcassette recorder. "Want to get started?"

"Yes, let's talk."

Leah activated the recorder. "I was thinking about your house, the one you grew up in. I'm trying to picture what it was like."

"Well, we lived in a couple of places when I was a child. My father, Pete Nichols, stayed with relatives when he first came over from Patras. His intention was to live in Washington for only a short while, and then go out to Colorado to work in the mines, as many Greek immigrants did. But he got a job in the market at Fifth and Florida Avenue, and soon opened his own fruit stand. He liked it here in D.C. He said he liked being close to the President and the Congress. 'I'm right here, in case they need my advice,' he said.

"My father married my mother, Evangelia, in 1899. It was an arranged marriage. She was sixteen years old.

I was born in 1900. I'm told we lived in an apartment in Southwest at the time. I don't remember that at all."

"What about the house on K Street?"

"Eight-oh-eight K, at Eighth and K, Northeast. Yes, that was the house my father bought for six thousand dollars."

"The house you were living in at the time when you met my grandfather," said Leah, helpfully. She had all of the information that Maria had just given her already, from previous interviews. She was trying to move things along. Her grandmother tended to forget their recent conversations, but remembered details from fifty, sixty years earlier with astonishing clarity. "Can you tell me about this house?"

Maria closed her eyes. She wasn't dozing. She was trying to see it. As Maria began to speak again, Leah took notes that she thought might be relevant to her upcoming project.

"It was a typical brick rowhouse with a front porch. Upstairs were three bedrooms and a bathroom. The bedrooms had gas jets for light. There was a garage back in the alley, but we didn't own a car. We lived with my grandparents on my mother's side. I had a little brother named Nick, but he died when he was five."

"I'm sorry."

"A lot of kids died back then, many from tuberculosis. Nicky died from diarrhea and enteritis. It was a common cause of death in children. His passing tore my mother up and I can guess that it hurt my father, too, but you wouldn't have known it. He was a can-do type. He liked to say that he only looked ahead."

"What else about the house? Describe it."

"Well, we spent most of our time in the kitchen. That's how I remember it. There was a furnace in the corner of the kitchen, and a truck would come through the alley and shoot coal into a bin. So we'd put a bucketful of coal into the furnace and that's what heated the house. Through the radiators.

"On one wall of the kitchen was a gas stove. On the second wall, a freestanding sink. On the third wall, an icebox. The iceman would deliver a big block of it and put it in the box using a pair of tongs. Ice on top, food on the bottom. In the winter we'd put our milk and butter outside, pass it through the window above the kitchen sink, right onto the sill. We shopped every day because the icebox was so small. We'd buy a live chicken from the market and my Baba would kill it out on the back stoop by cutting its neck. My grandmother would pluck the feathers, singe the chicken to get the rest of the feathers off, and then boil it. We ate at a big table that was also in the kitchen. In the early days I remember being hungry, but after my father bought his diner, there was always food. I worked at the diner in the front of the house until the time I was in my late teens. That's where I got to know your grandfather, Frank Brown."

"Where was the diner?"

"Fourteen twenty-Two H Street, Northwest. Around the corner from the White House." Maria smiled. "My father wanted to be as close to the President as possible. It was in the Woodward Building, right in the heart of D.C.'s Wall Street. I remember the chalkboards on the sidewalk, where the stockbroker assistants would change the numbers all day long. And we were on Newspaper Row. The *Washington Post*, the *Washington Times*, and the local bureaus of the *New York Times, Boston Transcript*, and the *Philadelphia Ledger* were all right there or around the corner on Fourteenth. It was very exciting for me to be around all of this as a teenage girl."

"How did your father get such a place? I don't imagine he had much cash."

"A banker took a liking to him. The banker gave him a loan based on a handshake. It was done in those days. My father went up to New York and bought the most up-to-date restaurant equipment. He was very proud of his place."

"What did it look like?"

"It was set up cafeteria-style. People slid trays down a line and got their food from steam tables, then paid the cashier and took their food to tables where they ate. Only my father and I were allowed to work the register. A kitchen was in the back where the food was prepared by a chef and his helpers. It was also where the dishes were washed. The dishwasher stood over two tubs, one holding soapy water, the other holding clean water. The dishwasher..." Maria hesitated, trying to recall something that had come to mind.

"What?"

"He was a Negro. His name was Robert Charles Weathers. I remember because, well, he was a striking man. Tall and well built. A veteran of the war. Soft-spoken. But when someone called him Robert, he always corrected them. 'My name is Robert *Charles*,' he'd say, in a quiet but firm way."

Leah wrote the name Robert Charles Weathers into her notebook. Something was familiar about the name, but how could it be? Why would she know the name of a man who washed dishes in the back of a diner, sixty years ago?

"I remember something else about Robert Charles," said Maria. "This was in the summer of 1919. Robert Charles came in to work one day after the race troubles had ended. His right hand was bandaged. My father never asked him anything about it. He said it was the business of the *mavros*, not his, though I think he knew why Robert Charles was injured. We just assumed he'd been involved in the riots in some way."

"What riots?"

"I don't recall the details, exactly. We had heard that a Negro man assaulted a white woman over by the Barracks. That's what started it all. The whole thing was awful and got very violent between Negroes and whites for several days."

"They prefer to be called Black now, Yiayia," said Leah, gently.

"But it changes all the time, doesn't it? Anyway, the riots were frightening, and we didn't talk about such things in my house. Negroes and whites worked together but we didn't mix or socialize. They had their own world and we had ours. They seemed content, to me."

Leah made no comment out of respect and instead changed the direction of the conversation. "You said you met my grandfather in the diner."

"Yes. Well, I actually met Frank Brown on the street one day while I was walking with his friend, Jack Donnelly. I was...I had started to date Jack Donnelly. I mean, I dated him first. Jack and Frank were business partners as well."

"What kind of business?"

"This was 1919, as I said. Prohibition had commenced in the District in 1917, over a year before it began in the rest of the country. Hundreds of bars and several breweries closed down, and thousands of jobs were lost."

"I don't understand the connection," said Leah.

"People wanted alcohol. Jack and Frank were filling a need. They provided liquor to the backroom speaks. They were bootleggers."

After some more back-and-forth, Leah saw that Maria was beginning to lose focus. Leah told her grandmother that she'd see her again soon. Maria studied Leah as she stood.

"You look very tired," said Maria. "Are you all right?"

"I was up pretty late last night and I couldn't get to sleep."

"You take care of yourself, honey. You're a lovely woman, don't ruin your looks. Even your name is beautiful.

Leah is a name out of Genesis, Hebrew in origin. A very common name for girls in Germany. Did you know that?"

"Yes, Yiayia. You've told me. Don't worry about me, I'll be all right."

After Leah had left, Maria folded her arms and settled in her chair. She didn't want to nap. It was pleasant to sit there and think back on her youth and those wonderful years.

———————

The first time Maria met Frank Brown, she was on the arm of Jack Donnelly. They were walking leisurely down 7th Street, window-shopping at the King's Palace department store, when they came upon Frank. Maria wore a beaded, baby-blue crepe dress. She stood straight to let Frank get a look at her. She was a lovely young woman and feeling it. Her full buttocks and strong legs filled out her dress.

"Well, hello, Frankie," said Jack, smiling brilliantly. "Maria Nichols, meet Frank Brown."

"Jack speaks highly of you," said Maria.

"And of you," said Frank. He produced a package of Chesterfield cigarettes and a box of Union matches, and gave himself a light. Later, Leah would come to know that Frank smoked more heavily when he was nervous or disturbed.

"What brings you down here?" said Jack.

Frank swept his hand around the block. "Shopping." He said it softly, as if he was afraid to be caught in a lie. It was the district for it, after all. Along with King's, there was Harry Kaufman's, Goldenberg's, and Lansburgh's, and all manner of tailors and haberdashers on 7th. Later, Frank would admit to Maria that he was wandering that day, as he had been feeling lonely. He'd gone down to 7th to kill some time.

"Gonna buy a suit, Frank?" said Jack.

Frank dragged on his cigarette and exhaled. "Oh, I don't know."

"There's plenty of Jew tailors down here who can fix you up."

"I guess I'm just looking around."

"We're going to lunch," said Maria. "Would you care to join us?"

Frank looked at Jack. Jack's genial expression had not changed, but his eyes said no.

"Thanks, but I've eaten," said Frank, another lie.

"We'll be on our way, then," said Jack, and he clapped Frank on the arm. "Tomorrow, right? Usual time?"

"Tomorrow," said Frank, turning to Maria and bowing his head slightly. "Very nice to meet you, Maria."

"You also," she said.

Frank stared into her hazel eyes.

Jack and Maria walked away arm in arm, as a streetcar passed and clacked along its tracks. Maria looked over her shoulder briefly at Frank, standing there, still looking her way. He was in a poplin shirt with a starched white collar, and wore gunmetal oxfords with a Yale toe. A sharp dresser, for sure. He was blond-haired, fair-skinned with blue eyes, and as tall as Jack, himself a big man. Frank was easy on the eyes, and clearly he was smitten with her. In another life she might have gone around with Frank. But she was with Jack. That is, she was at the time.

After lunch, Jack and Maria walked to Jack's pride, a 1917, four-cylinder Dodge touring car with black fender skirts, an electric starter, and wood artillery wheels. Jack was a sworn Dodge Brothers man. With Maria beside him, he put the stick in gear and pulled off the curb.

They drove north. 7th Street became Georgia Avenue, which until 1909 had been called Brightwood Avenue. Despite protests from local residents, the name change was approved in an appropriations bill sponsored by a Southern senator. The Feds controlled the city and could do as they wished.

Up on Georgia, people stood on a wooden platform, waiting to board an arriving streetcar. A horse, pulling a fruit cart, drank from a steel trough holding water on the side of the road. There was little motorized traffic on the street. Relatively few Washingtonians owned cars.

Jack parked on Quackenbos Street by the old Fort Stevens and the two of them walked onto the grounds. He told her, once again, about the Civil War battle that had occurred here and repeated the story of the President's visit during a skirmish and how, on that day, Lincoln had been fired upon. It didn't look like much of a fort anymore. More like an overgrown field of weeds and brush. Jack wanted to see a stone memorial that had been recently erected on the site. When they found it, he closed his eyes and crossed himself in the Catholic manner. Maria surmised that he was not praying for the Union soldiers who had died here and were buried in a small nearby cemetery, but rather for the Confederate dead. His sympathies went that way. Jack was a member of the locally formed Home Defense League. The group, an official militia, didn't like Negroes, in Washington or anywhere else. Jack often spoke negatively of their race. He was a supporter of President Wilson, who had enacted segregation in the federal government after taking office. Maria knew where Jack stood, but didn't like to discuss or think too deeply about his leanings. She mostly put it out of her mind. She wanted the relationship to continue. She hoped to marry him.

They next went to his place, a front-facing, furnished room with full electricity in a three-story house on Warder Street, Northwest, in Park View. Outside the door, in the hall, was a common bathroom and a wall-mounted phone.

Jack's bedroom caught the afternoon sun, but he had drawn the curtains earlier in the day, and the room was nearly dark. He lit a candle that was set on a basin next to the bed. He had filled the basin with fresh water and put a washcloth next to it that morning. He'd prepared for this, knowing they'd end up here sometime during the day. She'd known it, too.

Maria waited for him to come to her. Standing before her, he took her in.

"Did you wear that dress to church this morning?" he said.

"Yes," she said. "It's a little fancy, but I didn't choose it for the congregation."

The services for her Greek Orthodox Church, St. Sophia, were housed on the upper floor of Adas Israel, the first synagogue in D.C., at 6th and G. Land had been purchased for a freestanding permanent home for St. Sophia at 8th and L, Northwest, but the Great War had postponed its construction. Maria and her parents had gone to the liturgy in the morning, and then she told them she was spending the rest of the day with her friend Anna Katsouras. Anna would lie for her if need be. Maria said they were going down to the monuments and then to a movie, *True Heart Susie*, at the Savoy, one of the Crandall theaters, at 14th and Columbia Road.

"I chose the dress for you," said Maria.

"It's almost a shame for it to come off," said Jack. "Almost."

"Would you like me to take it off?" she said, boldly. It sounded like something a whore would say, but she didn't feel like one. She felt like a modern woman who knew what she wanted. She wasn't ashamed.

"Let me," said Jack.

He undressed her slowly and now she was clad only in her step-in chemise. She was trembling, not from fear, but rather from anticipation. When he took her in his arms, she felt him swell and pulse through the fabric of his trousers. The knowledge of what was to come made her heart race and her face warmed with blood as they kissed. The act didn't hurt anymore, not like it did the first time, *her* first time, when they had begun their love affair months ago. Now it felt like they were made for it and each other.

Afterward, they stayed in bed, Maria covered, Jack proudly naked atop the sheets. His spade-black hair was ruffled, and his brown eyes gleamed in the candlelight. Jack could be loud and aggressive, but when satiated he was calm and spoke more softly. She'd only been with him and didn't know what it was like with other men. She'd been warned by an older, more experienced woman who frequented the diner that a man will leave quickly once he's gotten what he wants. But Jack liked to linger and talk. Maria hoped this meant he was in love with her, though he'd never said so.

"It's not so bad here, right?" said Jack. "The room, I mean."

"It's nice."

"I'm going to get a proper apartment, with its own bathroom. That's next on my list. Me and Frankie are gonna grow the business."

"It's dangerous, isn't it?"

"Not too."

"You carry a gun."

"The Webley? That's for show. My Irish cousin gave it to me, like a present, when he visited last fall. Makes an impression."

She remembered the pistol. Jack had shown it to her. It broke from the top for loading. She'd never seen a gun like it before.

"Don't you worry that what you do is illegal?"

"Not at all. All I know is, I gotta work. The government shut the bars down, but also created an opportunity for guys like me. All those jobs lost, the tenders, the delivery men…We had to do *something*. Hell, I worked the stick on Rum Row on E Street, at Shoo's. Dennis Mullaney's, as well. I'd still be there if we hadn't been shut down." Jack turned to her. "People are always gonna drink. Don't your people like to drink?"

Maria chuckled. "My people?"

"Sure, the Greeks."

"I can't speak for all of them. I guess they do."

In her home at 8th and K, her father had made a trapdoor in the linoleum floor, covered by a woven rug. Beneath the floor they stored jugs of wine, homemade from fermented grapes. When she was still a child, before she grew too tall, he'd lower Maria into the crawlspace to retrieve and replace the jugs.

"Anyway, I don't worry about what's legal or illegal," said Jack. "I just work."

"What about your partner?"

"Frankie?" Jack grinned. "What'd you think of him?"

"He's nice enough, I guess."

"Yeah, he's swell. A little more cautious than me, but that's good. He keeps me in check. Frank's German, y'know."

"Oh?"

"You can tell by looking at him, if you're thinking about it. His parents are German immigrants. Frank changed his name. You wanna know what it was? Franz

Braun. When the war was heating up, there was all kinds of folks hating the Germans, and not just the ones over in Europe. American Germans as well. Hell, anti-German sentiment is one of the reasons Prohibition came about, what with all the German breweries. It's why Christian Heurich is selling ice now instead of beer. Me, I don't hate the Germans. At least they're white. So, yeah, Franz changed his name to Frank Brown before he enlisted and shipped out overseas. When I want to get under his skin, I call him Franz Von Braun. I like to rib him, is all."

"My family changed our name, too. It was Nikolopoulos. My father Americanized it to Nichols, and replaced the *k* with a *ch*. My father said it looked better when he made his signature. There is no *c* in the Greek alphabet, did you know that?"

"You don't say. I musta been absent the day they taught that in school."

Jack hardly asked after her family and when he did it was rote, without genuine interest. Sometimes she wondered what he thought of them. *Your people.* He had met her father at the diner, and they had gotten on all right, though her father eyed him with suspicion, as he did all men who showed any kind of interest in his daughter. If this was going to progress, if Jack and Maria were going to be permanent, it would have to be addressed. Jack had never broached the subject, or even mentioned that they might have a future together, but if it were to move forward, Jack and Pete Nichols would have to talk. She knew it was not going to be a pleasant conversation.

"Why so glum?" said Jack, who had noticed the troubled look that had come to her face.

"There's nothing wrong," said Maria. "I'm happy."

————————

Leah Brown lived in a house on Woodland Avenue in Takoma Park, Maryland, less than a mile over the District Line. She shared a basement apartment with Gary Shepherd, her boyfriend of many years. The owner/landlord, a quiet drug-addiction counselor named Dale, lived on the top floors.

Leah was thirty and Gary was thirty-one. They had met as undergraduates at the University of Maryland in College Park. Leah had graduated with a BA in English. Gary took film and lit classes but didn't earn a degree. They had bonded over their love of the arts, though neither of them had become artists. Leah, at least, was working on it.

She'd been a waitress at the Hamburger Hamlet on Democracy Boulevard for many years, taking the job during her freshman year of college and never really moving on from there. Gary had bartended at various spots in D.C. proper and was now at Mulberry Street Annex on upper Wisconsin Avenue. The restaurant/bar culture naturally fostered drinking and, as the '70s progressed, cocaine.

Leah and Gary started using coke recreationally but now it had turned the corner into something else.

A look at their checkbooks revealed register entries of $50 and $100 with increasing regularity. Most of their extra money went to grams and halves, and the habit had depleted their savings. Not that it had snuck up on her. She'd figured out early on that if you're using cocaine, you have a cocaine problem.

Entering her apartment, she smelled the heavy nicotine use from the night before, which meant they had been doing coke. Their coffee table held many empty beer bottles and a tire ashtray filled with butts. On the same table, a hand mirror had been licked clean. Record covers were scattered on the floor by the stereo. Gary had pulled out his second-wave ska albums, the two-tone bands Madness, the Specials, and the Selecter, as well as the English Beat's debut on the Sire label, and had played them into the night. Then they had rote sex and tried to get to sleep. This was the worst part of it for her. Her fists clenched, lying in bed, as the lightening sky seeped through their drawn venetian blinds. The sound of Gary snoring. The word *stupid* racing repeatedly through Leah's head.

They were too old to chalk up their cocaine use to youth and nearing the point where their professional prospects were narrowing. Gary still talked about becoming an artist, whatever that meant, but he had done nothing about it. Leah, a voracious reader, had wanted to be a fiction writer but as of yet hadn't even attempted it. Recently she had settled on the vague plan of writing a period novel set in Washington. The remaining people who had actually lived as adults around the early 1920s, the years in which she intended to set her book, were nearing the end of their lives. She wanted to take the opportunity to speak to them and get the firsthand facts she needed while she still could. The clock was ticking for her as well. She had accomplished little in her life so far, had noticed the lines that had begun to appear around her eyes, and had come to the realization that aging was real. If she was going to try this writing thing, the time was now.

Gary was preparing to head out to work. He'd been on the couch for most of the day. He grabbed his car keys from a bowl set by the front door. His jeans were hanging loose on his already thin frame, and his skin was pale.

"I've got to get out of here," said Gary. "I guess we overdid it last night."

"We should slow down," said Maria, her usual day-after comment. She meant *We should stop.*

"Yeah, I know."

"Gary. Before you go…"

"What?"

"Do you know the name Robert Charles Weathers? Why is that name familiar to me?"

Gary chuckled. "Are you kidding? Robert Charles Weathers is one of the top wideouts in the NFL. Unfortunately, he's with the Eagles and they're in our division. You've seen him shred the Redskins' secondary, that's why the name is familiar to you. He's a local product, was a big deal around here in the Interhigh. All-Met, in fact. He came out of Spingarn and went to Ohio State on a full ride. Now he's playing on Sundays."

"Right," said Leah. Of course Gary would know the name if it involved local sports. Gary was never an athlete but was a sports nerd, the kind of guy who'd been the statistician for his high-school basketball team. Gary listened to local legend Glenn Harris on WHUR's "Let's Talk Sports" with religious fervor.

Gary headed out the door.

The next day, Leah took the Metro down to the Martin Luther King Jr. Memorial Library at 9th and G, Northwest. It was there, at the city's central branch, that she did her research in the Washingtoniana Room on the top floor. Complete microfiche records of local newspapers gave her much-needed information for her research. As important as the articles were, more important were the advertisements and classified listings in filling out the details of the world she was attempting to build. For months now, she had been spending much of her free time in this room.

She retrieved the reels she thought she might need from the appropriate drawers, having gotten from Gary the month and year that Robert Charles Weathers had been drafted into the NFL. She fixed the roll to the spindle of the viewing machine, threaded the film through to the empty reel, and went to work. It was a long process, but she was diligent and patient. Two hours later she came upon an article in the *Washington Post* from 1977 titled "Three Generations of a Washingtonian Family Celebrate Robert Charles Weathers." The text detailed Weathers's path from Pop Warner to the NFL, his close relationship with his family, and the influence of Donald Mitchell, his football coach and English teacher at Spingarn High School. An accompanying photo showed Weathers in his draft suit, surrounded by Mitchell, Weathers's middle-aged parents, and his grandfather (also named Robert Charles Weathers), a tall old man leaning on a wooden cane. All of them were smiling triumphantly for the camera.

"Got you," said Leah.

She spent the remainder of the day reading old newspaper stories on the Washington Riots of 1919. It was all new to her, and fascinating. She printed out several of the stories. When she was done, the sky outside had begun to darken. She hadn't eaten or thought about it. She was stoked.

The following morning Leah phoned the office of Spingarn High and left a message for Donald Mitchell, young Weathers's former coach. She then worked a day shift at The Hamlet, and when she returned to her apartment that night received a call from Mitchell. She told him what she wanted, but he wouldn't address it until they met face-to-face. Leah agreed to meet him the next day in his classroom after the school day.

She entered Spingarn, a large brick structure on a rise on Benning Road in Northeast, the following afternoon. She found Donald Mitchell, a fit, bespectacled man in his middle years, seated behind his desk. The windows were open, which did little to alleviate the heat. It was still summer and the school year had recently commenced. Mitchell's classroom was adorned with inspirational sayings and portrait prints of Black authors such as Jean Toomer, Langston Hughes, Richard Wright, and Paul Laurence Dunbar, all of whom had spent time in D.C.

"Thank you for seeing me," said Leah. "I'm a little surprised you could meet me this time of day. I thought you'd be running football practice."

"I gave it up last year. I came to this school in 1960. Twenty years of coaching is long enough. But I still have a lot of work to do here in this room. Many of my students go on to college. I stay in contact with them after they graduate because they need it. Some don't make it past the first couple of semesters. There are money issues, and culture issues as well. So I keep up with them and give them the support they need. Other teachers and administrators do the same, it's not just me. But I felt like I needed to concentrate on that side of things going forward. I only have so much time in the day."

"I've heard this school has a storied athletic history."

"Well, famously, we graduated Elgin Baylor and Dave Bing, among others. The Green Wave is real. We got Michael Graham on the basketball squad now, and John Thompson's got his eyes on him. But this is also one of the best academic public schools in the District. The last segregated school built in D.C., two years before *Brown v. Board of Education*. The law changed, but...put it this way, you won't see any white kids walking these halls." Mitchell shifted in his chair. "Tell me why you're here."

"I was hoping to speak to Robert Charles Weathers's grandfather."

"You still haven't told me what you're up to, exactly."

"Like I said over the phone, I'm planning to write a novel. A historical novel set in the years around 1920. I've decided that it will be bookended by two major events that occurred here in the District. In my oral research I found that a few of my ancestors crossed paths with a man named Robert Charles Weathers. I'm hoping that this man is the grandparent of the young man you coached. The name is unusual. It can't just be a coincidence, can it?"

"I don't know."

"I'd like to get his perspective—"

"Hold up. You say you're planning to write a novel? *Are* you a novelist? Have you ever written one before?"

"No."

"I admire your ambition."

"Every novelist is a first-time novelist at some point."

Mitchell's eyes registered amusement. "You're bold, too."

"Can you put me in contact with him?" said Leah. "I read the article in the *Post*. I know you're close to the family."

"He's a tough old bird. Still angry about some things. He has a right to be. I don't know if he'll talk to you."

"Will you call him for me?"

"I guess you know I got a soft spot for writers. Even writers who haven't been published." Mitchell tented his hands. "I'll see what I can do."

———

It was two weeks before Leah met with Robert Charles Weathers. A series of phone conversations between them (and one canceled appointment due to what he said were health issues) had stretched out the time. Finally he agreed to a date. Leah's phone rang that morning but she didn't pick it up, guessing that he was going to put her off once again.

She drove out to Largo, Maryland, in Prince George's County. The house was a colonial with a two-car garage in a community with homes that looked, with small variations, alike. When Leah was growing up, PG County was mostly white and on the working-class side, but as she drove through the community she noticed a few Black residents out on their lawns or walking to their cars. It was a start.

She was let into the house by Lula Weathers, the daughter-in-law of the patriarch, and was shown to a sun-filled back room, where the elder Robert Charles Weathers sat in a recliner. The polished wood cane she had seen in the *Washington Post* photograph leaned against the chair. There were photographs of the grandson on the wall in his NFL uniform and in graduation robes, as well as framed commendations, uniform patches, and medals. A nineteen-inch color television was set on a stand, its remote Velcroed to the arm of the recliner. Clearly, this was where the old man spent his days.

He was dark-skinned, aged but not jowly, with a neat gray mustache and a full head of gray hair cut close to the scalp. She could tell he had been a handsome man by his deep brown eyes and the cut of his jaw. His legs had atrophied, but from the look of his thickly muscled fore-arms she could surmise that he had been strong. He didn't smile as she introduced herself. His handshake was firm.

Leah had a seat, pulled her microcassette recorder and her notebook and pen from her book bag. She asked him if it was all right to record their conversation, and he asked her why that was necessary. She then explained the reason for her visit.

"I'm only seeing you because Coach Mitch asked me to," said Weathers. "I wouldn't be inclined to, otherwise."

"I appreciate it, and I'll try not to take too much of your time. Just so you know, this is going to end up as fiction. No one will know your name or that you spoke to me. So if that is what concerns you, rest assured, you can speak freely."

"Humph," said Weathers.

He asked her if she liked the house, and she said that she did. He told her, with pride in his voice, that his grandson had purchased it for the family for thirty thou-sand dollars, cash. He said that in 1969 a woman had sued the builder of the community, who didn't want to sell her a house because she was Black, and that she had won the lawsuit. He said, "The woman stepped up, and that's why Black families are living here today. We still have to fight for our lawful rights." He said that his son had insisted he live with them here, and that he was still getting used to it.

"I always lived in the city," said Weathers. "This is country, to me."

"Where did you grow up?"

"In an alley. Willow Tree Alley, in Southwest. My people were slaves who came up from the South."

"The Deep South?"

"Southern *Maryland*—not too different. They worked a tobacco farm, even after Emancipation. But eventually my parents moved us up to the District. That's where I was born."

"Your family lived in an alley?"

"It wasn't uncommon. Alley homes faced each other and were in the backyards of street homes. We rented a house. Wasn't ours but it was a home. A kitchen with a stove, a toilet, a living room, and two bedrooms upstairs. I was the youngest of the children, and the four of us slept in one room. My father was a manual laborer, and the jobs weren't steady, so he was around most of the time. My mother worked every day because she washed clothes for white people, and there was always a need for that.

"The alley wasn't but thirty feet wide or so. We knew everyone, and in the summer especially, folks stayed outside. Cars couldn't come in and police rarely did. Some people had their own stills and sold corn whiskey. There was gambling and numbers, and there was fistfights and knives and families and love. It was what some folks would call a slum. It was our world."

"How long did you live there?"

"I left home at seventeen and started working in kitchens. Then I went off to the war."

Leah looked up from her notebook, upon which she had been writing. "When was that?"

"We shipped out of Newport News on March 30, 1918. First Separate Battalion of the 372nd Regiment. The First was all Black soldiers, going back to the Civil War. We went straight to France. By mid-April we were taken off the American command and assigned to the French Army. Became part of the 157th Division of Infantry. What they called the Red Hand."

"Why was your battalion separated from the American command?"

"I wasn't privy to the ins and outs of those kinds of decisions, but I do know that the white officers made it clear they didn't want us there. The colonel tried to transfer all of the Black officers out and replace them with white noncoms. That wasn't good for morale, right about the time we were heading into battle, but it also put a chip on our shoulders and made us strong. They didn't reckon on that."

"Where were you?"

"At various places on the Champagne front. My Springfield rifle and bayonet were my best friends. We took heavy casualties. Bussy Farm, Séchault, and then Trieres Farm. We didn't surrender or pull back. We had something to prove, and we did." Weathers pointed to the wall, where a framed, cross-and-sword medal on the end of a red-and-green ribbon was hung. "That's my Croix de Guerre. The French treated us right. They gave me that medal for valor. I was one of ninety-seven privates to receive it."

"Given how the Black soldiers were treated by the Americans, what motivated you to fight?"

"Pride. Like many young men, I was full of fire. I wanted to prove my manhood. And there was another thing, too. I knew if I got on that battlefield, I'd have the opportunity to kill some Caucasians. Does that bother you?"

"No," said Leah. But it did. "Want to take a break?"

"I'm okay if you are," said Weathers.

"So you went to work for Pete Nichols when you returned from overseas."

"Yeah. I didn't want to be a dishwasher, but at that point I would've taken anything. Wasn't like us Black soldiers got rewarded with chances when we returned to D.C. I was a reader, so I had a leg up on others. Was hoping to educate myself, because my schooling had been subpar. I didn't have the opportunities those brown-paper-bag, Dunbar types did. I'm talking about those folks who lived around LeDroit Park. Intellectuals and professionals. They say there's Black Washington and there's white Washington, but the reality is that there's two Black Washingtons. Do you understand?"

"I think so."

"Probably not, but let me go on. When I was a kid, I got a card at the Central Public Library, which was also called the Carnegie Library, at Mount Vernon Square. It was the first desegregated building in the city, so I could spend a lot of time there, just reading. I like history books, though even I knew that much of what I was reading, especially American history, was a distortion, and some of it was an outright lie.

"The library was the one place I felt safe in the city, outside of my alley. It was my sanctuary.

"Matter of fact, I had a book in my hand one day when I was walking on H Street, way downtown. Pete Nichols was standing outside his diner, smoking a cigarette. Short and stocky Greek with a brush mustache. He said to me, in a heavy accent, I'll never forget it, "How's it going today, friend?" I stopped and we talked for a few minutes and he got around to telling me that his dishwasher had quit that morning, and did I need a job. I never intended to stay as long as I did."

"I've been speaking with Maria Brown," said Leah. "Maria Nichols is probably how you remember her. She was Pete's daughter...she's also my grandmother. She mentioned you."

Weathers's face became animated with surprise. "She's still alive? I never would have thought she'd live this long, given that, you know..."

"Yes. Her husband passed. Did you know Frank Brown?"

Weathers nodded. "He was all right. Quiet. Not like his friend."

"Jack Donnelly?"

"I knew him as Jack, and only to look at. We didn't converse or anything like that."

Leah could tell from Weathers's tone that he didn't care for Donnelly and asked him why.

"I guess because I liked Maria. We weren't friends. A Black man didn't befriend a white girl back then. But she was kind in her dealings with me. So if she was good, I couldn't understand why she'd be around a man like him. I remember this one time, I was coming out of the kitchen to switch out a bus tray, it was peak time and everyone was busy, and I heard Jack say to Maria, 'You all are working like a bunch of niggers around here.' And when he saw me, and our eyes locked, his expression didn't change at all. I'm saying, he didn't care that I'd heard. I guess Maria was willing to overlook that side of him. People will do that when they're in love."

"I'm curious," said Leah. "Maria said that you insisted on being addressed as Robert Charles, rather than simply Robert. Your grandson also goes by Robert Charles. It must be important to you, but why?"

"It *is* important," said Weathers. "I was born in 1898. My father gave me my middle name three years later. He never did change it officially, but I was always called Robert Charles thereafter, and as a man I demanded to be called by that name. It was an honor to carry it. In the alley, when we were kids, we had heard about him. There were *songs* sung about the man."

"Who was he?"

"I'll tell you. Robert Charles was born in Copiah County, Mississippi, at the very end of the Civil War. One of the first free babies, born to sharecroppers who could read and write. Copiah was progressive in its time. Blacks and poor whites worked together under the banner of the Independent Party in an early version of racial solidarity, but as Reconstruction began to fail, the white Democrats down there destroyed those dreams through intimidation and violence. I say this because, later on, Robert Charles was called all kinds of things: 'savage brute, animal'… But he was a thoughtful man and in fact was part of the Back to Africa Movement toward the tail end of the century.

"As a young man he moved around plenty, looking for work, and ended up in New Orleans. One hot night in July, 1900, Robert Charles was sitting on the stoop of a house with a friend of his, relaxing and not bothering anyone. Three policemen answered a complaint about two 'suspicious-looking Negroes' who didn't look like they were supposed to be where they were at. You know how that goes. The policemen came and words were exchanged. No one knows exactly what was said but it's safe to say that a lifetime of being treated like dirt got Robert Charles's back up, and the situation got out of hand. Robert Charles had a gun in his pocket and drew it, and one of the police drew his, and they shot each other. Robert Charles, limping from a leg wound, fled.

"He went to his apartment and grabbed hold of his Winchester .38 rifle. Two police followed his blood trail there, and when they came to his door he shot them both dead.

"Robert Charles next hid out in a house on Saratoga Street and holed up there for three days. Meantime, the

Mayor offered a license to kill to any man who could get
Robert Charles, dead or alive. Riots commenced. Schools
and houses were burned and the rioters killed over twenty
people in their blood lust.

"The white folks in New Orleans were good at this.
They had practiced. Nine years earlier, white mobs
had lynched eleven Sicilian men and had walked away
uncharged for that crime.

"Robert Charles knew that he would be found, and
that he would be lynched without a trial. He had decided
to make his stand in that house on Saratoga and face the
mob with force. In the basement, he made his prepara-
tions. He fashioned bullets from a lead pipe that he melted
in the furnace, and molded them with a length of steel the
same diameter as the caliber of his Winchester. He waited
for his enemies to come.

"Eventually, they arrived. Militia, police, and citizens.
Some said there were over a thousand of them that surrounded the house. By now Robert Charles had gone up
to the top floor and had picked his firing positions well.
The mob fired upon the house, but Robert Charles was
not hit. Instead he chose his spots, moving from window
to window, and fired at his intended targets. He killed
another five policemen and militiamen, and wounded several others. Finally, a couple of men got into the first floor
and set fire to a mattress. Poured water on it so that it
would generate extra smoke. The house began to go up in
flames.

"Robert Charles came out of the house, Winchester in

hand, ready. He was shot right away. Then he got finished off from more gunfire. He was dead now, but they shot him again and again, with pistols and shotguns. They stove in his face. Dragged his body and made a show of what they'd done.

"It sounds like he lost, but he'd won. Black folks all over heard about his bravery and ignored the vile lies that got written about him in the newspapers. He took no one's shit. He was a man and he died a free man, on his own terms. That's why I'm proud to have his name."

"I can't begin to understand it," said Leah. "It's hard for me to listen to that story and take anything positive away from it."

"You can't see it from our perspective."

"I just don't know that violence is ever a good thing."

"No? People speak on World War Two as a good war. Necessary. What about the riots that happened in D.C., twelve years ago, in 1968? Sympathetic white people were content for change to come slowly, but when they saw what we were capable of, when they witnessed our capacity for violence, they got scared. Only then did change come quick. The Civil Rights Movement was accelerated by ten years in one weekend. I'd call that good."

"How about the riots in 1919? Did any good come out of it?"

"You know about that?"

"I've just begun to read about the event," said Leah. "My grandmother said you might have been a participant. Would you like to talk about it?"

"I'm not ashamed of it. But I'm tired."

"Can I come back tomorrow, same time?"

"Sure," said Robert Charles.

Before she left, Leah took note of an empty box of chocolates that had been discarded in the trash receptacle beside the recliner of Robert Charles.

She drove straight to the MLK Library and continued to research the events of 1919. There were five mainstream newspapers in D.C. at the time, and she realized that much of what she read was slanted against Black Washington—and, in a couple of instances, inflammatory. She did find some recently written articles about the riots that were free of editorial, and some period journalism in the *Washington Bee*, the city's Black weekly, and she printed those out and took them home.

Arriving in her apartment, Leah found that Gary had already left for his bartending gig that night. Her feeling of relief that she would be spending the evening alone was without guilt. Gary was a good person, but the passion between them was gone. Leah knew she had been prolonging something that she should have walked away from earlier.

The next day, she arrived at the Weathers residence with a box of Turtles—an irresistible mix of chocolate, pecans, and caramel—in her hand.

"That was nice of you, Leah," said Robert Charles. He

still didn't give her a smile but his eyes had lit up at the sight of the box. "Let's both have one before we talk."

They each had two.

Leah turned on her microcassette recorder and got her notebook and pen out of her bag.

"You need to understand the climate in D.C. at the time for Black Americans," said Weathers.

"I've been doing more reading on it," said Leah. "I know that the city changed when Woodrow Wilson was elected."

"First Democrat to win the presidency since the Civil War, and a Southerner in the bargain. He ran on a promise of 'New Freedom' but once he got in office he segregated the federal government. Before, there had been opportunity and advancement for us, at the Bureau of Printing and Engraving, and the Post Office, places like that. Folks who were on the way to being promoted got *de*moted. Black federal workers could no longer eat in the same cafeterias or use the same bathrooms as whites. They got put into what was called 'Jim Crow rooms.' There wasn't an official segregation law in the District, but we knew not to try and go into the changing rooms of white department stores, or white movie theaters, or white restaurants. The Klan had become a presence in Virginia and Maryland, and they had people in the city. And there was that Home Defense League...open racists. There were also thousands of white war veterans hanging around town, some still in uniform, unemployed and spoiling for a fight, 'cause these doughboys thought that any Black man who had a decent job here in D.C. had took that job from them. And here I was, I had fought for my country, and I was supposed to come back home and just accept that?"

"I understand your anger."

"Damn right I was angry. I still am."

Leah let him settle. "Tell me what you remember about the riots."

"I know that it was in July of 1919, and it was a Friday night. A white woman claimed that two Black men had assaulted her after she got off work in Southwest. Tried to steal her umbrella or some nonsense like that. Never has been determined what happened."

"I read that there had been a couple of rapes in the month preceding this incident," said Leah. "A Black perpetrator had raped and robbed a couple of white women in the city. The *Washington Times* called him 'a Negro fiend.' Was it possible that these incidents were all related?"

"This wasn't a rape," said Weathers. "And it wasn't that man who did those crimes. Never has been made clear exactly what happened that night. Could've been a simple argument, could have been physical contact...no one knows. But the woman's husband rallied a bunch of servicemen, citizens, and militia to find a suspect that they knew the police had questioned."

"The suspect was named Ralls," said Leah, after checking her library notes.

"Yeah, that's right. He came from Bloodfield, a rough old area known for bootleg liquor, gambling, and whorehouses. The mob marched toward Bloodfield and assaulted and beat down several Black people along the way. When they got to Ralls's house, Blacks and whites clashed. Guns got fired, and people were hurt. The police came and broke things up, but only for that night. They made no attempt to arrest any of the mob.

"The next day, Saturday, tensions grew all day. You could feel it. All kinds of white soldiers, Marines, sailor boys, and Home Defense League–types were talking about what happened the night before, and they began to gather and mobilize on that plaza on Pennsylvania Avenue, where the streetcar lines came together. That night they started beating on Black folks coming off the streetcars, and then the mob numbers grew as they moved into other parts of the city and beat, clubbed, and stabbed Black Washingtonians. This went on through Sunday, too, and into Sunday night. It was a bloodbath. But not just for our folks. For theirs, too. They hadn't figured that we'd fight back."

Leah knew that there had been violent racial incidents that whole year, all over the country. Charleston, Indianapolis, Wilmington, Knoxville...the burning of homes and properties, public lynchings...Black veterans shot to death, still in uniform.

"It was called the Red Summer," said Leah.

Weathers nodded. "In Chicago, Black folks put up a fight. So did Black D.C. Some called it a race riot. It was a *war*. I was right there in it. I *know*."

"How were you involved?"

"We set up a line of defense at Seventh and U. Folks had been buying guns from the pawnshops all that Saturday, when they could. Hundreds of them. More guns and rifles came in from Baltimore, too. I got hold of a Springfield rifle, same model as I had in the war. Me and this man Randolph, a sharpshooter I knew from the First, set ourselves up on top of the Howard Theater. We had heard that a Black girl had shot and killed a police detective who had tried to enter her home, and we knew that the retaliation would be fierce. But we were overdefended there, and at New Jersey Avenue. It wasn't enough action for me. I set out into the city with my friend."

"This was on Sunday?" said Leah.

"Monday. On Monday morning, the *Washington Post* put out some kind of statement, calling on all available military personnel in the area to mobilize and, you know..."

" 'Clean up,' the city," said Leah. "It's well-documented that the *Post* threw gasoline on the fire."

"I didn't go to work that day. I sent a cousin there to take my place in the kitchen. I didn't want to do Pete Nichols like that. He'd been good to me."

"What happened Monday?"

"All kinds of hell. The cavalry had been brought in from Fort Myer. There was a battle between police and citizens at Sixth and T. A police officer got shot and that meant it was going to get very serious. Never mind that the police had fired into the crowd first. I was around Ninth Street, way downtown, at the time. I had seen a Black woman get punched in the face by some young white man, and I jumped in. I beat that white boy 'til he was unconscious. His face was ruined when I got done with him. I broke three fingers doing it, and cut up my hand.

"There were battles on the edge of Bloodfield and at the Uptown line. People fought with revolvers, clubs, and straight razors. We held our ground." Weathers paused. "Something else happened."

"What?"

"I spied that man Jack Donnelly. He was part of the Home Defense League. I'd heard him bragging about it to Maria at the diner. And I came up on him and his kind on Monday night. Noticed that pretty Dodge of his was parked on the street. I saw Donnelly pistol-whip a boy, couldn't have been more than fourteen. Donnelly was twice that kid's size. I positioned myself at the corner of a building, not more than twenty-five yards away. I flipped up the sight on my Springfield and put him in the hairs of it. I knew that thirty-aught-six round would blow him up."

"Did you shoot him?"

Weathers shook his head. "Only because of Maria. But I've thought about it often. I would have had no regrets. I killed many men in France who'd done nothing to me. Killing a man like him wouldn't have bothered me one bit."

"You have a vivid memory."

"I'll never forget how it was. White men in cars, driving around town, shooting at us. Black folks beating white folks senseless. Thousands of troops patrolling the city, sent in by the President. That Monday we passed out guns among ourselves. You get a feeling, knowing that you're about to make a stand, that you're willing to kill and die for something important. Folks were scared, but it was a joyful time, too."

Leah thought of the casualties and the loss. The numbers had changed over the years, but no matter the exact details, the stats were grim. Two dead police. Also dead, forty-some whites and Blacks who'd expired on the scene, or later on from their injuries. Hundreds of wounded who'd made their way to area hospitals. Hundreds, mostly Blacks, arrested and jailed. The uncounted who went untreated and died in their homes.

"How did it end?" said Leah.

"Some said God, but you could also say Nature: it rained. A big summer storm came on Tuesday night and drove folks indoors. I think everyone took it as a sign. We were all tired, and it was time for it to end."

"Did it change anything?"

"Right away? No. But history is a continuum. Do you know what that means?"

"I think so. That all events build on each other."

"Close enough. There's no one event, it's all one thing. The past, the present, and then the future. Nothing changed right away after that summer. But those people who died defending their city and their loved ones were part of something that led to the Civil Rights Movement. Not saying our fight ended there. I won't live to see the end result of the struggle. But I know I played a part in it."

"Thanks for letting me listen."

"Felt good to speak on it."

"Can I come back?"

"Bring more chocolate," said Weathers.

Leah went back to her apartment, exhilarated. She had gathered valuable material and was beginning to "see" the fictional world that she was intending to create. She went to the bedroom she shared with Gary, where she had set up a desk. She began to listen to the tape recordings she had made and transposed the exact conversations, word for word, into a fresh notebook. This clarified some of the details she had hastily, originally scribbled onto the page, rendering them often unreadable, and guaranteed that she would get the words right before they faded from her memory.

That night, while she was still working, Gary came into the room to tell her he had scored a gram of coke. Leah was tempted, but knew that if she started in on it she'd be taken away from her work and be up most of the night. The first line of cocaine was the only good line, and after that you were chasing something that would end in frustration and regret. She declined. He told her he'd call a friend to come split it with him, and she said that was okay. Later, when she was in bed, and the music out in the living room had grown louder, she became annoyed, but also proud of herself for staying away from the drug, if only for one night. Lying there, she thought of the next visit to her grandmother, and the anticipation of discovering something new.

———————

"Take me into the early 1920s," said Leah, after activating her microcassette recorder. "After the riots."

Maria Brown, seated in her chair by her bed, folded her hands upon the afghan that covered her legs. Leah had closed the door of Maria's room so they would not be disturbed.

"Well," said Maria, "I was still with Jack. And I had… left home, and left my father's diner."

"Any reason for that, or was it just time to go?"

"My father had spoken with Jack. More of a confrontation than a conversation. My father didn't care for Jack for a number of reasons. He knew he was a bootlegger, for one. He told me, 'The guy's a criminal. A bum.' But mainly, I was his daughter and only living child, and he wanted me to marry a Greek. It was very unusual in those days for a young Greek woman to marry outside of our ethnicity and our faith. Not because we weren't attracted to other men, but because it was expected of us to stay with our own kind. My father and my mother were insistent that I follow that path. So one day my father and Jack had a talk, after the lunch rush in the diner. I was told to take a walk and I did. Their talk commenced. Jack later told me that my father began by saying, 'What are your intentions, sir'?"

"How did Jack reply?"

"I don't think he answered him directly. Jack told me that he said to my father, 'I care for your daughter and I promise to treat her with the respect she deserves.' I took that to mean that he didn't say he wanted to marry me, or even that he loved me. We didn't talk about it. At the time I thought that if I pushed Jack, I would lose him. And I didn't want that to happen. As for my father, he was not satisfied. He told me, 'If you keep this business up with the Irishman, you'll have to leave.' So I made a choice. I left.

"It was my father who had pushed me to take typing classes, to have a skill. So I knew how to type and got a job as an assistant for a lawyer who had an office around Dupont Circle. Then I got a private, front-facing room in a house on Kalorama Road for eighteen dollars a month. My pay was a hundred a month, so the rent was not a hardship."

"What about the relationship with your family?"

"That was difficult," said Maria. "I had lived with my parents and grandparents all of my life. I missed them. No daughter wants to lose her father's love. Not that he ever stopped loving me. But he was firm about his stance on Jack."

"You kept in touch with them?"

"Not directly. There was a confectioner store at 1203 H Street, Northeast, called Cokinos Brothers. The brothers, Peter and Adam, ran it. I had gone there all the time for penny candy when I was a child. After I became estranged from my family I'd visit the shop occasionally and talk to the brothers, get updated on what was going on with my parents. I think they did the same for my parents. It was a silly thing to do. We should have just spoken to one another directly, but all of us were stubborn. Anyway, that all changed, three years later. Everything did."

"Did your leaving the family move your relationship forward with Jack?"

"Not exactly. Jack treated me well. Took me to dinner, bought me things. One day we went down to Jelleff's on F Street, and he bought me a fox scarf with the heads still on. I still have it in storage. But as for moving forward? I assume you mean engagement or marriage. No. At the time I chalked it up to the pressure of his job. He and Frank Brown were running a full-on business, and it was fraught with problems."

"Bootlegging."

"Yes. There was always conflict. Jack and Frank paid off the police, as was standard practice. The Revenuers from the IRS were not so easy to slip, and they were a constant worry. And then there was the competition. Sometimes that got violent."

"Do you have an example?"

"Well, Jack told me once about an incident down on lower Fourteenth Street, at a blind pig owned by a guy named O'Brian."

"Blind pig?"

"A stripped-down, no-frills saloon. O'Brian was a friend of Jack's father, from when Jack grew up in Swampdoodle, the Irish neighborhood around North Capitol Street. Jack said that O'Brian's orders got lighter and lighter, until they dropped off to nothing at all. One day Jack and Frank decided to park on the street and watch the place. They saw two men carrying cases from a car up the stairs to where the bar was, on the second floor. Jack and Frank got out of Jack's Dodge and followed.

"They confronted the men. O'Brian was ashamed but he was being strong-armed. One of the men insulted Frank, calling him a 'lousy Kraut.' Frank didn't react. It was Jack who made the move. Jack pulled a gun on them, the Webley revolver that he carried while he worked. He told them he'd kill them both, right there on the spot, if they didn't leave and agree to never come back. Far as I know, they never did. I can imagine, the whole time, Jack had that tight-lipped smile of his while he threatened their lives. He could be very intimidating."

"Frank did nothing?"

Maria paused before she answered. "Frank was not a coward, if that's what you mean. He enlisted and served in France in the Great War. The Third Battalion, Sixth Marines. In fact, he fought in the Battle of Belleau Wood."

Maria thought back, to the only time that Frank had opened up to her about his war experience, late one night, late in his life, when he had been drinking. Belleau Wood had been taken and held, but it was one of the most brutal battles of World War I.

"No, Frank Brown was not a coward. He just didn't care to fight anymore."

"Did Jack Donnelly serve?"

"Jack served stateside. I often think that, had he seen

the war close up, he might have been less of a violent man. But I'm speculating, you know. We never spoke of such things."

"You were with Jack, but...forgive me, it sounds as if you were close with Frank as well. After all, you did marry Frank..."

"Yes," said Maria. "We married."

Maria saw the young Frank in her mind. He'd been taken with Maria from the first time he met her, down on 7th. He'd come alone to the diner, before she'd left it, and sit there and watch her work. Smoking his Chesterfields, because he was nervous. Another *xeni* suitor to make her father angry, but Pete Nichols was more concerned with Jack.

The three of them, Jack, Frank, and Maria, spent more and more time together, driving around in the Dodge, and walking along the banks of the Potomac and the Washington Channel, in that natural, ungroomed area that would later become Hains Point. Going to the movies together, because Maria loved the silent pictures, the orchestras, and the ornate theaters. It was obvious to Maria that Frank was in love with her. But it didn't seem to bother Jack, or, more likely, he simply didn't know. He wouldn't have believed that his best friend would be after his girl. He wouldn't have seen it. And after all, why would Maria ever look at another man when she had a strong, handsome specimen like Jack? His confidence had made him blind.

As for Maria, she had also begun to have feelings for

Frank. Maybe it was because Frank was more attentive, and Jack was increasingly distant. Eventually, around Christmas, a cold December night, 1922, after Frank had met her and given her a present, a cameo brooch on a gold chain, her resistance broke. She was curious and she boldly kissed him. And then Frank took Maria to his room on Lamont Street, where they made love. It happened only once. As a lover, Frank was a gentleman. If anything, too much of one. Maria preferred the roughness of Jack, the way he handled her and dominated her in bed. As for Frank, she wasn't ashamed of what they'd done. She thought of herself as a modern young woman. Her body was hers. She could make her own decisions with it, and do with it as she wished. She was fond of Frank, but she was in love with Jack.

"Is there anything you'd like to say about that?" said Leah.

"I think not," said Maria.

"I apologize if I overstepped."

"It's okay. But I prefer to hold some things private."

"I understand. Would you like to go on?"

"Tomorrow, dear. I'm done for today."

Leah returned the following afternoon after calling in sick to cancel her restaurant shift. She had been reading about the events of 1923 deep into the night, and was ready to move forward.

Leah sat beside Maria Brown in the room, Maria in her usual chair. The Olympic microcassette recorder had been turned on. Leah had closed the apartment door.

"You said that Frank Brown gave you a present around Christmas, 1922," said Leah. "Let's move on to the next month: January 1923."

"You want to talk about…"

"Yes. If you're up for it."

"I don't mind," said Maria. She looked toward her window, which gave onto a view of the woods that bordered the facility. "Okay, let me…"

"Take your time."

Maria folded her hands upon the afghan blanket. "A snow began to fall on January twenty-seventh, a Friday. It was a light snow at first, but it grew heavy during the night. By Saturday afternoon, the snow had accumulated considerably. It was well over two feet in the city, and I believe it measured thirty inches in Rock Creek Park. Washington automobiles and streetcars were paralyzed, but the snow was beautiful, and many adults and children of course were out in the streets. By nightfall on Saturday, the snow had pretty much stopped coming down. Nothing but flurries.

"Jack had moved to Park Road, I was on Kalorama, and Frank's place was on Lamont. All of us lived near the center of Adams Morgan. We decided to go to the movies that night. Jack and Frank knew I loved the silents and they were, as always, willing to please me. Jack picked me up and we walked down to the Knickerbocker, one of the

Crandall theaters, where Frank met us outside the ticket booth, at Eighteenth and Columbia Road. That night the feature was *Get-Rich-Quick Wallingford.*

"Anyway…the Knickerbocker was a beautiful, opulent theater, with a large balcony. It held seventeen hundred seats, but that night, because of the snowstorm, it was not anywhere near capacity. I suppose that was a blessing. But there were many families there. Women and children.

"We found our seats, about twelve rows back from the screen. I was between Jack and Frank. Jack was to my left. I don't know why, but that was our usual seating arrangement when we went to the pictures together. It had begun to get complicated between the three of us at that point, I've already told you why. Jack didn't know about what had happened between me and Frank. He certainly would have confronted us if he did. There had been a little bit of tension earlier in the evening, maybe because Jack was tiring of Frank always being around. But it seemed to have dissipated by the time we entered the theater.

"In the intermission, Frank said he was going out to the lobby to have a cigarette. He left Jack and me in our seats.

"Jack put his arm through mine. He leaned into me and gave me a soft kiss on my cheek. Then there was a hissing sound, and a great roar. I looked up. The ceiling of the theater split open and my life changed forever. Someone screamed. I suppose there were many screams. I saw objects falling toward me. When I regained consciousness…"

Maria stopped talking.

"Let's take this slow," said Leah.

Leah had already done the research. She had first read the *Washington Post* article dated January 29, the source for many of the subsequent news and magazine pieces that would detail the tragedy. The piece carried no byline but was written by John Jay Daly, the *Post*'s drama critic at the time, who had attended the showing that night but had emerged uninjured. The salient facts were this: the roof of the Knickerbocker had collapsed under the weight of the snow. Tons of steel, wood, plaster, and concrete came down upon the audience. The balcony sheared off and entombed those seated below it. One of the theater's brick walls also fell.

"When I regained consciousness...I know things now, I've read extensively about the tragedy, as have you."

"Tell me what you remember. At your own pace."

"I woke to darkness, and the sounds of moaning. Children crying, and begging for help. I looked up. There was no roof. It was open sky. Flurries were drifting down. There was a great deal of pressure upon my legs. Pressure, not pain. I couldn't seem to move. My right arm was free and I reached down and felt a block of concrete that was covering my waist and thighs. I whispered, "Jack," and turned my head to the left. Jack's body was crushed and he'd...his head was not...he'd been decapitated."

"I'm sorry. Let me get you some water."

"It's not the first time I've talked about this. Let me go on while it's on my mind."

Leah knew the grisly details. Rescue workers and fire-men arrived after navigating the snowy streets, and got to work. Their lanterns lit the room. The kettle drums of the orchestra were used to carry out debris. Except for the lucky who had sat near the exits, and those in the lobby, few of the theater patrons escaped death or injury. Panicked citizens searched through the twisted steel, torn timber, and heavy rubble for friends and loved ones. Most had been partially buried. Priests said prayers over corpses and gave last rites to the dying. Girders and beams had broken through the masonry instead of supporting it, rendering them lethal. Saws and acetylene torches were used to cut through the heavy wire screen that had failed to fortify the plaster ceiling. Whole rows of theatergoers had perished. Entire families had been killed in seconds. Nearby churches became makeshift morgues. There were ninety-eight dead. One hundred and thirty-three had been seriously injured. The scene was as grim and horri-fying as the aftermath of a battlefield.

"I blacked out again," said Maria. "What I remember next is Frank crouched over me. He was trying to hold his emotions back, but the fear on his face was plain. There were tear tracks on his face. He was gripping my free hand and telling me that everything would be all right. His eyes said that he didn't believe it. He told me he loved me. He tried to move the concrete off of me and he couldn't do it. He asked me if it hurt and I said that I couldn't feel much of anything at all, and that made his anguish worse. He turned his head and screamed for help and no one came. He told me he was going to get someone and that he would be right back. He left. I went to sleep."

"What do you remember next?" said Leah.

"I woke up in Garfield Hospital," said Maria, and she looked down at her legs. "The night I walked into the Knickerbocker auditorium and took my seat was the last time I took steps. I never walked again."

The room fell silent. Leah looked away from Maria, sitting in her wheelchair by the bed.

———

Leah asked a fellow waitress to cover her next few shifts at The Hamlet. She had gained momentum and wanted to speak once more to both Maria Brown and Robert Charles Weathers. Though she would probably stop her fictional story at the Knickerbocker Disaster, she owed them the courtesy of allowing them to talk on about the subsequent years. Also, she had become interested and invested in their lives.

Leah brought flowers to Maria Brown and put them in a vase on the nightstand beside her bed. As she had throughout their interviews, she turned on her recorder.

"In broad terms," said Leah, "tell me about your life after 1923."

"It wasn't as bad as you might expect," said Maria. "There was the heartbreak of knowing the permanent extent of my injuries. The adjustment. But...good came out of it, too."

"You mean, your relationship with your parents?"

"Yes, there was that. My parents and my grandparents were at Garfield Hospital every day that I was there. I awoke to the sight of them, and Frank. My father was in my life again, completely, until his death. A few months after the accident, when I had come to terms with my handicap, my father put me to work again at the diner in The Woodward Building. Taking cash as I had always done, with some modifications to the base of the register, courtesy of Baba. I worked there until the children came."

"My father being one of them."

"Yes, Jack. Named after Jack Donnelly, of course."

"When did you marry Frank Brown?"

"Nineteen twenty-five. I tried everything to get him to change his mind, but he was not to be denied. And my father never said a word about him not being Greek. In my father's mind, Frank had saved my life."

"When did you start to have kids?"

"Well, I couldn't bear children myself. We adopted our first child in 1930. Named him *Friedrich*, after Frank's father. We always called him *Fred*. And then, Jack, your father, came to us a couple of years later. You and your siblings have not a drop of Greek or German blood in you. Neither did our children. But we loved them deeply. Of course there are many different ways to make a family."

"My dad still talks about Uncle Fred."

"Jack idolized him."

"Fred was killed in Korea, wasn't he?"

Maria nodded. "He enlisted in the Marine Corps,

as his father had. We tried to talk him out of it, but he wanted to follow in his father's footsteps, as sons do. That was another useless war.

"After Fred died, Frank began to drink more heavily. He had always liked his drink, but it became a crutch. Being in the bar business as he was, it was an easy trap to fall into. He got into owning drinking establishments after Prohibition was lifted. He had a couple of places around town. It was a cash business then, no credit cards, so we hid most of our money from the tax collectors. Some of that money went to my daily care. I had live-in help in our house, a Negro...a *Black* woman named Almeda. Frank provided everything that I needed. He was devoted."

"He sounds like a saint."

Not a saint, thought Maria. He had his affairs. One of them had been a longtime lover. She had phoned their house one night, drunk, asking for Frank. Maria had hung up on her. Frank didn't think Maria knew, but she did. She had lost the use of her legs, but not her sense of smell. Over the years, Maria had accepted Frank's indiscretions. She and Frank couldn't have sex together, certainly not intercourse. Frank had his needs. But he had always come home after closing time. So, no, he wasn't a saint. Just a man.

"He loved me, always, and I loved him. He died many years ago."

Leah remembered it. She was fifteen years old when he passed.

"He went out to cut the grass in our backyard and

had a massive heart attack. He was found lying next to the lawn mower. He was a lifelong smoker, and I guess it caught up with him. I miss him."

"What about Jack Donnelly?" said Leah. "Do you miss him, too?" It was an inappropriate question but this was family history that went beyond her research. She wanted to know.

"It was so long ago. In some ways it doesn't seem real. I will tell you this: when I was in the theater, pinned beneath that concrete, and I saw that Jack had been killed, I felt...no grief. I know it sounds cold. I've thought about it often, with some degree of guilt. But at that moment, I was only thinking about my own survival. Praying that someone would come and save me. It's human, isn't it, to feel that way?"

"Yes. You don't seem bitter about what happened."

"The Knickerbocker Disaster was a tragedy, but it was no one's fault. Nature met physics, and nature won. Many people suffered, not just me, and not just the dead and their loved ones. The architect of the theater, Reggie Geare, was legally absolved of any responsibility for the collapse, but his reputation was destroyed and he died by suicide. Harry Crandall was also cleared of any wrongdoing, and he continued to operate his theaters for a long while, and even built new movie palaces in the District. But the Depression ruined him, and he killed himself as well."

Leah had read about it. In the hotel room where Crandall died of self-induced gas poisoning, he left a note for reporters:

Don't be too hard on me, boys. I'm despondent, and miss my theater so much.

"You're quite a survivor, Yiayia."

"I'm like most people," said Maria. "I'm still here, and determined to be here for as long as I can manage it. You see, there was nothing but infinite darkness before I was born and there will be the same forever when I pass." She leaned forward and put her hand over Leah's. "You say you want to write a novel? Then stop talking about it and write one. This is all…" She made a sweeping motion of her hand.

"I get it. I do."

Maria's eyes grew distant. "Leah is a name out of Genesis. It's Hebrew in origin. Did you know that?"

The next day, Leah Brown sat with Robert Charles Weathers in his sunny room at the back of the house in Largo. They were drinking coffee and grazing from a box of chocolates she had brought that morning. Weathers's son, Ivan Weathers, a sharply dressed man in his late middle years, had answered the door and led Leah back to the room.

"I spent more time with Maria Brown," said Leah. "Do you remember when she came back to work at the diner, after the Knickerbocker Disaster?"

"Sure. That was a happy day for Pete. I should say *bittersweet*. His daughter was back in the fold but she was never gonna be…I mean, she was crippled for life."

"Do you remember the Knickerbocker Disaster?"

"Remember it? Shoot, I was there."

"What?"

"Not in the theater. Wasn't any Black folks in the theater, not on that or any other night. At the time the roof collapsed, I was over off of U Street, east of 16th, seeing a young woman I knew, the same woman who later became my wife."

"What put you at the theater?"

"Well, news traveled fast then, over what they called 'the city telegraph.' I wasn't far from Adams Morgan, so I walked up there to see what I could see. It was chaos. The ambulances and fire trucks couldn't even get in close enough to do their work. Soon as I arrived I got put to work with six, seven other men, all of us Black. They tasked us with shoveling out the snow.

"At one point I saw Frank Brown, coming out the theater, yelling at anyone who'd listen that he needed help to get someone out. We only knew each other by sight, but had never spoken. I started to get out of the shoveling line to go in there with him, but a police officer told me to stay where I was and keep working. That I was needed there, that I'd do more good behind the shovel. Then two white men who had some size on them stepped up and followed Frank back into the theater. Soon after Frank carried Maria outside in his arms and put her in an ambulance. She wasn't conscious that I could see. She was pale as milk."

"What else do you remember about that night?"

Weathers paused. "That night? Wasn't any whites or

Blacks. We were all Washingtonians. It felt that way to me. But of course that spirit of brotherhood didn't last."

"Did you ever tell Frank Brown you were there?"

"Wasn't any reason to. I did see him a couple of times after that, over the years."

"When?"

Weathers thought it over. "Well, 1932. Me and about twenty thousand World War One veterans, Black and white, from all over the country, went down near the Capitol and pitched tents. We were concerned that a payment to veterans, like a bonus, which had been promised to us, was in a bill that was gonna get killed by the politicians. They called us the Bonus Army. I saw Brown outside a tent there, but again, we didn't speak." He chuckled. "Don't you know, we never did get that bonus. Most of us went home, but a few thousand diehards stayed in those tents, and had to be evicted with tear gas and tanks. General Douglas MacArthur was in charge of that cleanup operation. Imagine him, strong-arming veterans. I never did care for that man.

"The next time I saw Frank Brown was after the Second World War. I don't recall where it was. I was on the street and he was getting out of a cab, about to go into a nightclub. Might have been Club Kavakos, on H Street, Northeast. A woman was on his arm, a shapely and hard-looking blonde."

Leah nodded. Her grandmother had said as much.

"Did I step over the line? I'm talking about your grandfather, I know."

"No, I want to hear everything. How long did you work for Pete Nichols?"

"Till Pete sold the place in The Woodward Building, right before the war. Pete bought a place near the Greek church at Eighth and L. Since most of his customers there were Black folks, he learned to cook Southern. What people later called soul food. It was a beer garden at night. I visited him once or twice. Saw his obit in the *Post* about ten years ago."

"What did you end up doing for a living?"

"After I left Pete I went to work as a driver and delivery man for a liquor distributor. Did that for several years. I got friendly with one of my clients, a Jew named Rosenberg, who owned a liquor store on Georgia Avenue, in Park View. He offered me a job behind the counter. After the schools got desegregated by law, white folks started moving uptown, north on Georgia, and eventually over the line into Maryland. Mr. Rosenberg bought another store west of Rock Creek Park, and kept the one in Park View, but he didn't want to work there anymore. He made me manager. Rosenberg was a decent man. I didn't have ownership in the store, but I was well paid, and he set me up with health insurance and a pension plan. It was enough for me to buy a house in Hillcrest Heights and raise my family. I was at the shop until he sold the business and the property; I was close to seventy. And here I am, an old man."

"You're not so old."

"Oh, but darlin, I am." Weathers smiled at her for the

first time since they'd met. "No one really wants to listen to me anymore. I enjoyed our conversations."

"So did I."

"I don't know if you're ever going to write that book of yours. But people sure do need to be taught their history. Promise me that someday folks will read about the things I told you in this room."

"I promise, sir."

"Call me Robert Charles," said Weathers. "I insist."

"I know you do," said Leah Brown.

Leah Bagdasarian had frequently heard that the great riddle of life is what happens to us when we die. In reality, the greatest mystery is the passage of time.

I'm seventy-three years old. I am old.

Her age was an astonishment, but a constant one, as she was reminded of it every day. In the careful way she moved, so as not to disturb her fragile back. By the music she heard, more window-rattling bass than melody. Technology she had tried and failed to keep up with, because, why? Mostly, the turn of events in her country, the reversion of rights that others had fought for long ago. There were so many things to remind her that she didn't quite belong in this world anymore.

And yet, she wasn't ready to go. She had friends, she had grown children who checked in on her regularly, grandchildren who sent her cards on the appropriate days.

She no longer worked for a paycheck but she volunteered in a soup kitchen. She lived independently. No nursing home (they were now called assisted-living facilities) for Leah. She wouldn't have a death like her grandmother Maria, dehydrated and deliberately starved in the "health center," in a sterile white room, attended to by indifferent strangers.

No, Leah wanted to die in her apartment in The Chancery, on Wisconsin Avenue, near the National Cathedral and St. Sophia, the Greek Orthodox Cathedral at 36th and Mass. In her own bedroom, the musty smell of the place around her, her African violets set by the window, the photos of her children, grandchildren, and ancestors on tables and the walls.

Her husband, Paul Bagdasarian, was gone. Not dead but gone. He'd wanted to "explore other possibilities," which meant he was jettisoning the baggage of an aging woman so that he might enjoy his sunset years in the company of females twenty years his junior. Predictably, he'd moved to Florida and, contrary to his fantasy of enjoying a single life of multiple partners, married quickly and settled into a gated golf community, where he lived among people his own age while his younger wife, her skin the texture and shade of beef jerky, wore tennis outfits and a sun visor and rode around on an electric cart. She was just nice enough, and Leah did not dislike her. Paul had the money to feed his "lifestyle" and enough to ensure that Leah would live out her days in comfort as well. When she saw him and his wife at family holidays, he put on a hale and hearty front, but Leah knew him well enough to see that he was suffering from buyer's remorse. Paul had wanted his freedom but he had simply walked into another cage.

Leah didn't feel vindicated by his ennui, and she wasn't bitter about his exit. In fact she was content.

She'd met Paul in the Washingtoniana Room of the MLK Library, where she'd gone to work after earning an advanced degree in library science. Her employment there was a natural progression for her, as she had simply enjoyed being in that room and, later, helping people with their research. Having split with Gary, she was still single when she noticed a dark-haired, handsome man on the green side of thirty, sitting at one of the microfiche projectors, scrolling through old newspapers. Sometime that day he'd come to the desk, where he asked a fellow librarian, a somewhat snooty woman named Helen who'd been there for years, why his books were not included in the collection of local fiction authors.

"What books?" said Helen, in a condescending way.

"I'm the author of two Washington-based novels," he said. "My name is Paul Bagdasarian."

He was dressed in a black shirt, jeans rolled at the cuff, and high-top black Chucks. He was not indignant at all, but rather soft-spoken.

"Write down your name, legibly," said Helen, as if she was speaking to a child. "I'll look into it."

After Paul Bagdasarian had moved away and was wandering the nearby stacks, Helen said with a short barking

laugh, "Can you believe that guy? He says he's an author."
Her voice was loud.

Paul emerged from an aisle, looked at Leah and Helen
with both embarrassment and disdain, and left the room.
Leah could tell that he had overheard Helen's crack. She
followed him out into the hall and caught up with him at
the elevator bank.

"Hey," she said.

Paul turned to face her. "What is it?"

"You're an author?"

"I said as much. Your co-worker finds it funny."

"I apologize. Helen thinks authors should look a certain way. Like, you should be wearing tweed and carrying
a pipe."

"I get it. I'm young."

Leah paused. "You're not *that* young."

"Kettle black," said Paul, and thankfully for him she
smiled.

Paul returned to the library the next day, and the
next day after. He said he was researching his next book,
but she knew he was there to see her. He was interested
and so was she. He was of Armenian descent, and that
appealed to her, as Greeks and Armenians were practically related, though, as her grandmother had pointed
out to her, Leah had not a drop of Greek blood in her.
But she was building a case for him in her mind, and
to her it was one more thing in his favor. They both
loved books, local music, and films. Both of them were
drug-free after having wrestled with cocaine habits.

They were good together in the bedroom. Two years later, they were married.

Paul's first couple of novels were Steinbeck-inspired tomes of working-class Washingtonians, without the permanence of that writer's best work. They didn't cause a ripple in the publishing pond and he knew he was in danger of having a short literary career. He began to write thrillers, the madman-in-the-Pentagon, plot-to-kidnap-the-President type of thing. The books were competent, devoid of art, formulaic, and deliberately dumbed down for mass consumption, but the pages were easily turned. His intent was to return to more serious fiction later on but he was making too much money to turn back and he never did. It happened for Paul, but not in the way he had planned. He knew his books were disposable but his wealth had grown and in fact his kids would be millionaires upon his passing, and there was that. He had provided in a big way.

As for Leah, she wasn't bitter about her own unrealized literary ambitions. She had written the novel she had planned to write, and it simply didn't work. She supposed she knew it while she was writing it, but she doggedly completed it. She then attempted to get an agent but couldn't manage to summon up any interest. So she sent the manuscript, un-agented, to several major and small-press publishers and got one reply, a short and not especially encouraging rejection letter. This was all before she met Paul. She never tried to write fiction again and was satisfied to spend her working life in a library.

Secretly, she was proud that she had written a book.

Leah had kept the manuscript. She was looking at it now, three hundred and eighty-five pages, rubber-banded atop her file cabinet. The title page read *Knickerbocker.* Next to it, a manila folder filled with paper, labeled ORAL HISTORIES, WASHINGTON, 1919–1923. She picked the folder up off the file cabinet, grabbed her car keys, and left the apartment.

Leah drove her Honda CRV across town, stopping briefly to look at the site of the Knickerbocker Theater at 18th and Columbia Road. After the disaster, a movie theater called The Ambassador was built in the Knickerbocker's shell. The screen eventually went dark but in the 1960s the space was converted to a "psychedelic" club featuring short films, music acts, and the sale of black lights and marijuana paraphernalia. The Jimi Hendrix Experience played The Ambassador for five straight nights in August 1967. Hendrix set his Strat on fire at the conclusion of each set. Tickets were $1.50 during the week and went up to $2.50 on the weekend. The club closed the following year and shortly thereafter caught a wrecking ball. The site was now the branch of a national bank. Leah stared at the bank, wondering how many, if any, remembered what had stood there in the past.

She continued on her way and parked in a City Center lot near Mount Vernon Square. She walked to what had been the Carnegie Library, now the home of an Apple Store as well as the Historical Society of Washington, D.C.

The beaux arts architecture and façade had been preserved, with the addition of Apple's corporate logo.

Her father's diner in The Woodward Building was now a white-tablecloth restaurant. His soul-food place uptown was the site of two-million-dollar condos. RFK Stadium had been torn down. Spingarn High School was permanently closed.

If you stay in one place long enough, thought Leah, *your own city will begin to haunt you. Buildings vanish, the elders pass, and as generations proceed the deceased are forgotten.*

But not quite yet. Leah was keeping a promise. She was set to donate her oral histories to the Washington Historical Society for an upcoming exhibit detailing the 1919 Washington Riots and the Knickerbocker Disaster.

Her contact at the Historical Society was a young woman with a punkish haircut and a small diamond stud in her nose. She led Leah to a glassed-in room where they could spread the materials out on a table.

"Let me clarify the names of your participants," said the woman, pen in hand. "It's Maria Brown and Robert Weathers?"

"Robert *Charles* Weathers," said Leah. "That's correct."

OWNING UP

HE'S IN THE back seat of a brown-over-brown, '72 Mercury Marquis. Though it looks like a family sedan, long and spacious enough to hold five passengers in comfort, it is powerful (heavy, not fast off the line, but mightily powered), with a 460 V8 and a four-barrel carb under its hood. Nikos's father bought it the previous year at that dealership on Colesville Road in downtown Silver Spring, the one with the tiny showroom. The Marquis falls between a Ford LTD and a Lincoln Continental in the Blue-Oval family. It's not quite a Lincoln, a car that his father has always coveted but will never acquire.

Nikos, the family's only son, is wearing a blue blazer with attendance pins affixed to the right lapel. The jacket is too small for him and his wrists scarecrow out of his shirt. Nikos studies the veins popping out at the top of his forearms and those worming his hands. *I'm getting strong like Dad.* He's noting the changes in his body as his blood ticks up with anticipation, thinking of the house at the northwest corner of 16th and Van Buren, *that house*, which they are nearing now. Seeing it, a fieldstone mansion that since January has carried the aura of a dark fable told around a campfire, excites him. Death is still an abstraction to him. He doesn't fear the void but rather romanticizes it in the way that some boys his age tend to do. Nikos is thirteen years old.

His father is driving south on 16th Street, the Avenue of the Presidents, his mother, Helen, in one of the three dresses she owns, seated on the big velour bench beside him. It's Sunday morning, and three-fifths of the Tzirimis family (Nikos's two older sisters are in college) is on the way to church.

"There it is," says his father, meaning *that house*.

"Jim," says his mother, mild admonishment in her voice. "Do we have to? On a Sunday?"

"Your man Lew Alcindor paid for it," says Jim, ignoring her, cocking his head toward his son in the back seat.

Nikos doesn't correct him and say "It's Jabbar." His father knows about the name change, it happened years ago, but he still calls the man Lew Alcindor to rib his son. Nikos has a customized white T-shirt that he sometimes wears when he is playing pickup. On its back he has written the name Kareem Abdul-Jabbar and the number 33 in green magic marker, a hero-worship his father finds amusing since Nikos is on the short side, even given his age, and he's white. Nikos does not think his father is a racist (which is to say he doesn't know what's in his father's heart), though it's clear he doesn't like "certain kinds" of Black people. His father was okay with Martin ("a good man") but not Malcolm ("a troublemaker"), and he rooted for Frazier over Ali (a "loudmouth"), but that's predictable as in general he is resistant to most types of change.

"He bought the house, Helen," says Jim. "Alcindor did. For those people, whatever they are."

"They're Muslims, Dad," says Nikos, who has read about the event in the *Washington Post*.

"Yeah, I know," says his father. "So?"

"It's a religion."

"Oh, really? What kind of religion says it's okay to murder women and children?"

If Nikos were older, if he knew more, he'd mention the Crusades, or the Holocaust, but at this point in his life he can't rebut his father because he doesn't read many books, and religion is not taught or discussed in his public junior high school. He knows only that Muslims are "the other," which is really what his father is saying, too, in his own way.

"Jim," says his mother. "Can we *not*? It's horrible, and I don't want to talk about it on a Sunday."

By now they've gone down the long slope of 16th past the House, and they're crossing Military Road. Beyond Military, just below the tennis courts and the Carter Barron Amphitheater, they'll turn and enter Rock Creek Park, where eventually they'll branch off Beach Drive onto Klingle Road and come out into the upper-strata neighborhoods ("West of the Park") that seem so exotic and unattainable to Nikos, and take Reno Road south to their church. There Nikos will half-listen to the liturgy and observe the rituals (kneeling, doing his stavro on cue), not knowing what the words mean, and mingle with his friends during coffee hour, and he'll forget about the house at 7700 16th Street (which people have taken to calling "the Hanafi House," or "the Murder House") until next Sunday, when Nikos and his parents again pass it in his father's car. At which time Nikos Tzirimis will get that same familiar feeling of dread and excitement, both of those sensations at once, that many Washingtonians who lived in the city or in its suburbs, in that era, feel to this day, when they look at the fieldstone mansion that sits on a slight rise like a giant tombstone, a house that surely must be haunted by the ghosts of the dead.

When Nikos is older, he'll research the Hanafi House murders, knowing that some of what he reads (because it's coming from the internet) might not be the truth. By then he knows that the written word is simply the writer's truth. And yet, in all of the articles and postings, there seem to be common facts. Here is what Nikos thinks is a reasonable summation of the event:

On January 18, 1973, a mass murder occurred in a fieldstone mansion at 7700 16th Street, Northwest,

Washington, D.C. Two adults and a minor died of gunshot wounds. Four children ranging in age from nine days to ten years were forcibly drowned. Three were found floating in a bathtub; the infant was drowned in a sink. The minor, an eleven-year-old boy, was shot to death in a closet. Aside from the two adult fatalities, two other adults were shot and survived.

The house had been purchased by Milwaukee Bucks superstar center Kareem Abdul-Jabbar and donated to Hanafi Muslims for use as the "Hanafi American Mussulman's Rifle and Pistol Club." Jabbar had no connection to the massacre or to the murderers, though for some time he would be unreasonably tainted by the killings in the public's eye. He was a pallbearer at the burials.

The intended target of the attack, Hamaas Abdul Khaalis, was not at the residence at the time of the carnage. Khaalis, born Ernest Timothy McGhee, converted to Sunni Islam and joined (some say infiltrated) the Black Muslims, becoming national secretary to Elijah Muhammad at the party's Chicago headquarters in the latter part of the 1950s. Khaalis, as a Sunni Muslim, believed that the religion of Islam is color-blind and that the Nation of Islam had changed the doctrines of the faith when they excluded whites and accepted Elijah Muhammad as the messenger of Allah. This caused a falling-out between Khaalis and Muhammad's Nation of Islam. Khaalis moved to Harlem, created his own site of Hanafi/Sunni worship, and tried to persuade other Muslims to defect from Muhammad. Khaalis converted Jabbar, who then bought the $78,000 mansion and donated it to the Hanafi sect as their Washington, D.C., headquarters. In the meantime, Khaalis had sent letters to fifty ministers of the Nation of Islam accusing Elijah Muhammad of deceit and robbery. Khaalis's conflict with Elijah Muhammad triggered the former's death sentence.

The executioners of that sentence were seven members of Philadelphia's Black Mafia, who traveled to Washington, D.C., on January 12. All but one had done time in Pennsylvania's Holmesburg Prison and had violent criminal records. All seven self-identified as Muslims. In fact, they were little more than murder-for-hire hitters.

On January 17, the perpetrators arrived at the house in separate cars. Two of them entered under the ruse of wishing to purchase Hanafi pamphlets and literature. The man who answered the door, Khaalis's son, Daud, went to retrieve the material, and when he returned he found five more men had been let into the house by the first two. A slaughter ensued.

(Years later, when Nikos talks about the massacre, over drinks or around a dinner table, or in interviews, he leaves out the details of the murders, out of respect for the dead. He himself is a father and can't bear to talk out loud about the specifics of what occurred in that house, especially what happened to the children. He doesn't even care to think about it. In this way he is most like his mother, who later in 1973 asked his father to take a different route to church on Sundays so they would not have to drive by the house at 16th and Van Buren.)

The killers left incriminating clues, including fire-
arms, and were easily apprehended. One of the men
charged, James Price, entered a witness-protection program in exchange for his promised testimony. But when
the trial commenced he refused to testify after Minister
Louis Farrakhan issued a slightly veiled warning to him
in a radio broadcast. Price, convicted for an earlier, unre-
lated killing, was later slain at Holmesburg Prison, where
he had been housed on the same block as Black Muslims.
His death was regarded by law-enforcement officials as
an assassination. Half of the other defendants were convicted. Of the remaining three, one died of leukemia after
his conviction, one was acquitted when Price refused to
testify, and one was the beneficiary of a mistrial. In the
mind of Hamaas Abdul Khaalis, the American justice
system had delivered no closure or satisfaction.

Four years later, in 1977, Khaalis would return to
Washington to exact his own brand of justice.

It's a warm day on March 9, 1977, very warm, the ground
is still hard from the winter freeze, but people are walking the streets in shirtsleeves. Not unusual for the D.C.
area. Nikos is in his Problems of the Twentieth Century
class at his high school in East Silver Spring, in Montgomery County, a couple of miles over the District Line.
It's an elective he takes in his senior year to get himself
to graduation. His schedule this year is first-period Gym,

then Bachelor Living, POTC, and English, the only subject he's interested in and the only one he does well with because he gives a shit.

The English teacher, Mrs. Bolus, has told him that he's a good writer and he should pursue it. He doesn't know how to go about that but he likes the feeling of being praised for something. Only the English teachers in his schools, from junior high on, have shown him any kind of positive attention. He's never seen a guidance counselor, not once. He doesn't know what he's doing after graduation but his father has told him that he's going to college. He guesses it will be Montgomery Junior College (MJC, "Harvard on the Pike") or the University of Maryland at College Park, which is cheap (less than a thousand dollars per semester) and easy to get into if you're in-state. Nikos is not worried about it.

At seventeen, Nikos is of average size and build, still on the thin side. He's grown into his body and his nose. His car is a light-blue-over-blue '67 Plymouth Belvedere coupe with a 318 V8 (not too fast but respectable, a workhorse Mopar engine). His father accompanied him when he bought it off a used lot in Petworth for $499, paying for it with the money he'd saved from his job. It's got nice lines. There are no dents, rust, or Bondo on its body.

Nikos played on the soccer team for three years. He was unremarkable and unskilled, was not a starter, and was used primarily as a warm body and for his ability to slide tackle. ("Go in there and take him out," says the coach, a math teacher who took the job for the extra pay.) Nikos got what he wanted out of it: a letter and letter jacket.

Nikos likes girls, one in particular, a black-haired Jewish girl named Mindy Goldman, who is his on-again/off-again throughout high school. She's pretty and has the body of a woman, and sometimes he thinks he loves her, but occasionally he'll find out she's been with other guys, jocks who are better athletes than he is, or that one dude in high school who owns a Vette, and that has been what has broken them up in the past. But they've survived those bumps in the road and still see each other.

Nikos is into music and concerts. His first live show was The Who at the Cap Center when he was thirteen. He went with a friend and his older brother. Lynyrd Skynyrd opened for The Who (the Quadrophenia tour) and blew Pete, Roger, Keith, and John off the stage. He's since seen Skynyrd solo at the same venue, along with Sabbath, Uriah Heep, BOC, Deep Purple, and others. He saw Yes and ELP there and both times he fell asleep as his pot high wore down during the dreaded drum solo. He saw Zeppelin at the Baltimore Civic Center, one of the biggest thrills of his life, and J. Geils at the same venue. He caught Black Oak Arkansas at the Kennedy Center one snowy night. Because of what the raucous crowd did to that hallowed venue, the Kennedy Center never held another hard-rock concert again.

All of that is to say that he's a normal public high school kid on "the other side" of Montgomery County (it's not upper-income Potomac or Bethesda), though he doesn't feel normal. He's having fun but his head always seems clouded. It's like his brain continually needs to be rewired. Years later he'll figure out that this feeling *is* pretty normal for a boy his age. But to him, in those years, it just feels like confusion.

His day in school ends after four classes. He's walking out of the building, headed to his car, on the way to his job, when he sees a kid named Barry Rosen who is much smarter than him but for some reason is always eager to talk to Nikos.

"Hey, Nicky," says Barry, bespectacled and somewhat overweight, as he doesn't get any kind of physical exercise.

Barry Rosen has a small circle of friends who smoke pot on Saturday nights, sit in someone's basement (no girls within miles), listen to *The Dark Side of the Moon* in its entirety or the second side of *Trans-Europe Express*, and then play Risk. Barry's heading to MIT in the fall.

"What's up, Barry?"

"You hear what's going on in D.C. right now?"

"No, what?"

"A bunch of Muslims raided the B'nai B'rith building this morning and they're holding hostages. And then some other Muslims got into the Islamic Center and are holding hostages there."

Nikos knows what B'nai B'rith is because Mindy's father works there in some capacity.

"Why would Muslims take over the Islamic Center?" says Nikos.

"It's a *faction* of Muslims," says Barry, using a word

Nikos does not entirely understand. "The same ones whose family members got slaughtered in that house on Sixteenth Street a few years ago. That's what the guy on the radio said, anyway."

"Oh." Nikos knows that house well.

At this moment Nikos sees Mindy coming out of their school, accompanied by the sole security guard. She's crying. Nikos goes toward her but the security guard, a big guy named Mr. Garr, puts up his hand in a halt sign.

"What's going on, Mindy?" says Nikos, who obeys Garr's command and stays in place.

"My father's been taken hostage."

"Is everything all right?" says Nikos, ineffectively.

"I don't *know.*"

"Leave the young lady alone," says Garr. "She's got to go now."

"Call me at work," says Nikos.

Mindy barely nods as she heads for the gold Chevelle her parents bought for her on her last birthday.

Nikos finds his Belvedere and cooks the ignition.

———————

Heading south on Georgia Avenue, crossing the District Line, passing Morris Miller's liquor store and that corner diner with the facade shaped like a coffeepot, Nikos finds a station playing the news on his AM car radio. Details are spotty and coming in bit by bit. Nikos will discover exactly what is happening over the next two days. He'll write about it years later.

At around eleven in the morning, several men, under the direction of Hamaas Abdul Khaalis, entered the B'nai B'rith building at 16th and Rhode Island Avenues, Northwest, carrying shotguns, handguns, and machetes. There were a hundred people in the building at the time. Sixty-five of them—including Mindy's father, Sam Goldman, a public relations man for the organization—were taken hostage, while the remaining occupants barricaded themselves inside their offices. The intruders, who announced themselves as Hanafi Muslims, threatened the hostages with murder (decapitation, specifically) if their demands, as yet to be announced, were not met.

About an hour later, two armed Hanafi men entered the Islamic Center of Washington and took eleven hostages, a group that included employees and Muslim students who were visiting the center.

No one had been harmed at that time. The worst was yet to come.

———

Nikos works part-time at Payless Appliances and Mattresses on Georgia Avenue in Brightwood. It's a small shop that is well below the caliber of local chains like George's, Sun Radio, and Luskin's-Dalmo, and even below the next tier, mom-and-pop operations like Frank Slattery's place in Bethesda. Payless is owned by Mortimer Bender, a World War II veteran, and his two brothers, Irv and Phil, all raised in the District and all graduates of Central and Roosevelt. The Bender brothers are actually in the real estate business, buying up buildings at fire-sale prices after the '68 riots and white flight. The store isn't a front, it makes a profit, but it isn't their main source of income, which is property management and investment. Payless sells reconditioned major appliances, televisions, and mattresses bought on the cheap. The goods can be purchased on time at a high interest rate. The showroom is overcrowded with merchandise and haphazardly staged, giving it the appearance of a cut-rate, third-world market. That is the idea.

Nikos parks on Sheridan Street and walks up to the shop on Georgia. He likes this commercial strip of Brightwood, partially for its heavy population of Greek-owned businesses and its holdout population of Greek-American residents. There's the Greek market on Underwood, and on Georgia the Arrow Cleaners, owned by the Caludis Family, and John's Lunch, a diner owned by John Deoudas, and The Sheridan movie theater, which plays second-run pictures most times but on Wednesday night shows Greek-language films programmed by Penny Apostolides, a local entrepreneur who has her own radio show in town. There is another thing that Nikos likes, too: he works in the for-real D.C., not in the white, west-of-16th-Street D.C., and it gives him bragging rights with his friends. In his mind, working in the city makes him seem tough.

A small bell hanging over the door announces Nikos as he enters the shop. Edwin Taylor, clean in his tailored black slacks, pointed burgundy dress shoes, and vanilla-colored, textured Banlon shirt, is seated on the edge of a console TV, smoking a Kool, watching a news feed on a live TV that is up on the shelf among several others. Ed is a Korean War veteran in his forties. He walks with a slight limp from the grenade fragments lodged in his hip. He is street-lean. He is a smart but not trendy dresser. He keeps his natural cut low and his mustache scissor-trimmed.

"Ed," says Nikos.

"Nicky."

"Where's Ray?"

"Out back, I expect, getting his head up."

Nikos nods at the live television, where an image shows a reporter outside the B'nai B'rith building. The TV is a coveted Sony, and it lives up to its reputation as having the best picture, so it's the one they keep on during the day in the shop. Even used, the set is not cheaply priced.

"I heard about what's happening," says Nikos.

"Those Muslims took two buildings now."

"My girlfriend's father is a hostage."

"Damn. I hope he's all right 'cause they're not playing."

Ray Baumann comes into the showroom via the back door leading to the alley. The alley is where he smokes pot from his one-hit pipe. Ray stays high all day. He frequently offers to share it with Ed and Nikos, but Ed doesn't get high and Nikos won't smoke at work on account of the respect he has for the boss, Mort Bender.

"The Greek has arrived," says Ray, ripped as Cheech and Chong put together, though aside from his pink eyes it's not obvious. When Ray is high he just feels normal. It grounds him, somewhat, from the over-caffeinated version of his straight self.

Ray's smiling and his lank black bangs have fallen over his forehead. He's wearing threads that were tired when they still carried their price tags. His shoes are scuffed and his clown-knot tie has stains on it. Ray spends most of his earnings on rent, beer, weed, and alimony (when he pays it).

"What's the latest?" says Ray.

"The Muslims took the *Is*-lam Center now, too," says Ed.

"You don't want to fuck with those A-rabs," says Ray. To Nikos he calls them "Dune Coons" but never when Ed is around.

"Nicky knows one of the hostages at the B'nai B'rith."

"My girlfriend's father," says Nikos.

"For real?" says Ray.

"That's what Mindy told me," says Nikos. "She had to leave school, that's all I know."

"I hope he's okay," says Ray. And then, predictably, he says, "Because if your little Jewess gets sad about her pops she might not put out for you. That's one nice piece of trim, Jim."

There's a lot to process in that statement, but Nikos, at this point in his life, isn't equipped to unpack it.

Ray Baumann is thirty-two. He is twice divorced ("The first one didn't count"), with two little boys by Lynn, his second wife, a good woman who left him because it was not in his nature to be faithful. He sees the boys every other weekend. He's got issues with Jews and Asians, and assorted foreigners in general, but not with Blacks, with whom he professes to feel a kinship.

Ed has Ray's number. Mort Bender (whom Ray will often call "that cheap Jewish prick," even though Mort hired him, pays him a fair hourly wage, and gives him a commission on his sales) deliberately put a Black guy (Ed) and a white guy (Ray) on the sales floor because the clientele is mixed, increasingly leaning to Black. This doesn't stop Ray from stepping up to take the Black customers and then "talking Black" to them during his pitch: "That's a baaaad TV set, Jim, I kid you not." Some of them buy it and the rest of them know he's a bullshitter and patronizing them, but for the most part they're well-mannered enough to let him run his mouth. Ed hasn't called him out on it yet.

So Ray calls people Jim in the manner of an early-1960s white hipster trying to be street. (On this Ed corrects him: "My name is *Ed*.") Ray seems to have missed the second half of the last decade. He didn't get drafted for Vietnam, claiming his number never came up. ("I didn't even have to pretend I was queer," says Ray; Ed says to Nikos, "You know Ray was 4-F, don't you?") As for his active role in the summers of love, Ray does mention that he got some of that "airtight hippie poontang" on a trip to San Francisco and says that he saw Hendrix at The Ambassador in 1967 (many Washingtonians lie about this one, just as they will lie in years to come about witnessing Bruce's three-night stand at The Childe Harold in '73), but he doesn't recall any of the songs that Jimi played.

Ray has to tell anyone who will listen, after he says his last name, that "I'm German but not a German Jew. I know Baumann *sounds* Jewish, but…"

This is where Ed, who's a reader, says, "You know what the German derivation of the name Baumann is, right? It means peasant."

"It means farmer," says Ray.

"Same thing," says Ed.

"Now you're gonna get all high and mighty. Don't forget, your people picked cotton."

"Yeah, but they didn't *want* to, Adolf."

Ed has seen Ray's driver's license and Adolf is Ray's actual middle name. Given that Ray's parents were third-generation German-Americans, and that they gave Ray his middle name while Hitler was still in power (albeit when der Führer was in his last days in the bunker), it is kind of odd that they would bestow that reviled tag on their only son. Maybe that's why Ray never speaks about his parents. When Ed mentions the Adolf thing, Ray goes uncharacteristically quiet or simply says, under his breath, "Fuck you, Edwin."

Ray is a garden-variety loser but Nikos doesn't see it

that way. He's willing to overlook all the negatives (well, most of them) because he likes Ray's hustle and style. Plus, Ray has been nice to him and taken him under his wing since he's worked at Payless, while Ed has been kind of chilly at times. It's not a stretch to say that Nikos looks up to Ray. Nikos's best friend, Tony, an Italian kid he's known since childhood, who's book-smarter than Nikos, met Ray once and said, "That guy's your Fagin." Nikos doesn't know what that means.

A call comes into the shop that a truck is nearing, and Nikos meets the driver out in the alley. Thankfully the guy is delivering only a few television sets (portables, not consoles) and two mattresses, so the work is fairly easy. Nikos unloads and handcarts the goods by himself, then places the TVs on the shelf and connects them to a coaxial cable at the direction of Ed and Ray. They don't help him, even when he's struggling. It's Nikos's job to do the physical work in the store, after all. And to clean the place when he is not otherwise busy, and to take the merchandise out to the customers' vehicles and load them up after the sale. He is sometimes tipped for this and on occasion delivers the merch himself if the location is in the neighborhood. He works here five days a week, comes here after his half day of high school, and it gives him pocket money that most of his peers don't have. Hanging with Ed and Ray in the city makes him feel like an adult, like he's in on something that his friends are not.

Ray and Ed do their own ticket writing, credit apps, and cashiering. Mort Bender had tried out a couple of young women at cashier, but with Ray around they had targets on their backs. In truth Nikos got involved with one of them himself. Mort saw the legal issues in all of this, and the moral as well, and he stopped hiring cashiers.

After the truck is gone Ed asks Nikos to run across the street to John's Lunch and pick up some food. Nikos does it, returns, and gives the food to Ed, who doesn't thank him for the service. It's just the way Ed is.

Ray is finishing up with a customer, an older Brightwood resident wearing a cap jauntily. He's about to walk.

"This is for my grandson," says the man, indicating with his hand the Zenith TV set that Ray is pitching. "He doesn't need a new one, it's just for his dorm room at college. But y'all's prices aren't that good. I can buy a new set for forty dollars more."

Ray ignores that. "This unit comes with a ninety-day warranty, of course. Parts and labor, like a new set. And I can extend that warranty for you, too: $19.95..."

"If the set's any good, why would I need a service policy? What can you do about the price?"

"It's rock-bottom, sir. *Rock*-bottom."

"I think I'll look around. Thanks for your help."

The customer leaves. Ray is loath to cut the price to save a sale, something that he is authorized to do. It eats into his commission, for one, but he says, "It's the principle of the thing, too," whatever that means.

Ray comes to Ed, eating his lunch, and Nikos, who is standing beside him. They're watching the latest news on the Sony.

"Guy wanted a dis-count," says Ray, who has the need to explain his inability to close. "I mean, the set is used. We're already giving him money off. That Zenith's a dog, but you know what I say: 'Payless, *get* less.'"

"Shut up, fool," says Ed, who has put down his cheeseburger. "Trying to listen to this."

"What's going on?"

"They took over the District Building," says Nikos.

"The Muslims?"

"Now they went and killed someone," says Ed.

They pass the afternoon and early evening watching the news. Few customers come in, and the ones who do want to talk about the day's events or join Ed, Ray, and Nikos in front of the Sony. The city has been virtually shut down, and the monuments have closed, along with many government offices. Nikos phones his parents, who urge him to leave the shop and come home. But he says he's okay and stays until closing time. Mort Bender stops by to see how everyone is doing. He's attentive to Nikos, there's a bond there for him because the Greek and Jewish cultures are similar and because Nikos's father, like Mort, is a World War II combat veteran.

"We're closed tomorrow," says Mort, a tall thin guy with swept-back hair, graying on the sides. "Same as always. Just as well. This thing doesn't look like it's going to end tonight, so everyone should stay safe at home."

Payless closes every Thursday. It's the day Mort and his brothers meet to go over the books of their various

businesses, and since the shop is open Saturdays he likes
to give his crew two days off a week.

After Mort leaves, Ray approaches Nikos.

"Say, Nicky," says Ray. "What are you doing tomorrow, after school?"

"I dunno."

"You up for an adventure?"

"Like what?"

Nearby, Ed is listening.

"I got this friend," says Ray, "name of Bradford. Brad's
sweet on this little high-school gal who works up at the
Arby's in Wheaton. She had this boyfriend for a while,
older dude, a real creep, lives in an apartment out in
Springhill Lake in Greenbelt. She thought he cared about
her, see, so she took all of her records out to his crib, on
account of they were spending so much time together and
they both liked to listen to music. Anyway, this old creep
dumped her and now he won't give her back her records."

"Isn't your friend *Bradford* kind of old to be going after
a high-school girl?" says Ed. "If he's your friend he must
be close to your age."

"So what?"

"That makes him a creep, too."

"Mind you own business, Grandpa. You're old as Blac-
ula your *own* self."

For this Ray earns a rare smile from Ed.

"What do I have to do with this?" says Nikos, now
interested.

"Me and Brad are going to get back that girl's record

collection. I need you to drive. Brad doesn't own his own vehicle and neither do I at this moment—"

"'Cause your car got repossessed," says Ed.

"Yeah, it got repopped, so what? I've been going through some tough times, what with the divorce…"

Ed chuckles and shakes his head.

"You guys are going to break into this guy's apartment?" says Nikos.

"The girl's still got a key. The creep gave it to her. So it's not a break-in."

"Yes, it is," says Ed.

"I don't know," says Nikos.

"Look, you like music, Nicky, I *know* you do. You got that compact stereo down in your bedroom. You probably listen to music all the time, when you're not jacking off to that *Playboy* you keep under your bed."

Nikos is thinking, *How does Ray know about that?*

"Here's the deal," says Ray. "You can choose as many records as you like and keep them. Brad can just tell his little girlfriend that the old creep threw some of them out."

"I gotta think about it," says Nikos.

"Call me tonight and we'll firm it up," says Ray.

As they turn out the lights in the shop and prepare to lock up, Ed says to Ray, "Aren't you gonna ask me to come along?"

"Why?" says Ray.

Ed says, "I like records, too."

At home, Nikos is at the kitchen table with his mom and dad watching the news on their thirteen-inch black-and-white GE television set, complete with rabbit ears and a UHF loop antenna. The unit sits atop a metal cart on wheels. Nikos has missed dinner but his mother has reheated the stuffed tomatoes she served earlier. They sit here in the kitchen every night after they eat and watch television, although his father has a Sylvania twenty-five-inch color console down in the family room. They enjoy this time together.

They're watching the news, which has gone on past the regular hour.

This is what they know:

At 2:40 that afternoon, after the taking of the B'nai B'rith building and the Islamic Center, two shotgun-wielding men entered the District Building, overpowered the desk security guard, and rode the elevator up to the fifth floor, where Mayor Walter Washington was conducting day-to-day business along with his staff. Upon exiting the elevator, the men began firing their shotguns. One of the blasts struck twenty-four-year-old WHUR News reporter Maurice Williams in the back, killing him almost instantly. D.C. Protective Service Division Officer Mark Cantrell was shot in the head and would die a couple of days later. One of the pellets ricocheted and struck young D.C. city councilman Marion Barry in the chest. Barry, bleeding profusely, made it to a city council room that was in session, and collapsed. He was removed from the building via a window an hour later. His wounding and survival would add to his growing legend and help propel him to the mayor's office two years later.

The Hanafi Muslim intruders took hostages. As in the B'nai B'rith siege, many, including Mayor Washington, stayed safely barricaded in their offices.

It soon became apparent that Hamaas Abdul Khaalis was behind the day's events. He had been stewing, collecting weapons, and making plans since the slaughter of his family members in the house on 16th Street four years earlier. Khaalis soon made himself visible, denouncing the Jewish judge who had presided over the killers' trials, and the "Jewish-led press." He wanted the killers of his family delivered to him so that he could exact his own revenge. He wanted the killers of Malcolm X. He wanted to speak to Muhammad Ali. He wanted movie theaters to stop playing *Mohammad, Messenger of God*, a film recently released in major markets, a picture he deemed sacrilegious. He wanted to be repaid $750 in fees for a contempt-of-court citation he had earned during the trial.

Much of this was relayed via phone calls to Max Robinson, a Channel 9 news anchor, who, along with his co-anchor, Gordon Peterson, had become an institution in Washington. Robinson was Black and Khaalis felt he could trust him.

"That man's crazy," says Nikos's father, Dimitri, who goes by Jim.

"Those people he hates did kill his family," says his

mother, Elaine, who will usually try to inject something positive into the debate. "Anyone would be upset."

"He wants them to stop playing a *movie*," says Jim. "And he wants a seven-hundred-and-fifty-dollar refund for a ticket he got in court. Those kinda demands make the whole thing seem silly, don't they? For an Anthony Quinn movie his guys murdered that young reporter?"

"It's more than that," says Nikos, but it's just a feeling he has and he's got nothing to back up his argument. Plus, he knows that his father is right: Khaalis *does* seem crazy.

"I see he didn't call on your guy Jabbar for help," says Jim. Nikos's father no longer calls Jabbar Lew Alcindor. It's been a slow evolution for Jim Tzimiris, but it has come.

His father has never been vocally negative about Black people or the Civil Rights Movement, which is to say that he has not infected his children with hate like the parents of many of Nikos's peers, and yes, that is something. Jim has a small diner downtown with a longtime all-Black crew. He pays them a fair wage and gives them health insurance and they've raised and supported their families because of the job and stayed with Jim for many years. So when a liberal lady in the neighborhood chastises his father for mentioning that he was "talking to a Black guy the other day about what he thought of Jimmy Carter" ("Why do you have to say that he's Black? Can't you just call him a man?"), Nikos looks at her and thinks, *What have you ever done for anyone, Black or otherwise, except run your mouth?*

"Jabbar is a religious guy," says Nikos. "But he's not

into any kind of violence. He's done with those guys, I think."

"Politics and sports don't mix," says Jim.

"Have you heard anything about Mindy's father?" says his mother.

"I called their house but no one picked up," says Nikos.

"Those idiots haven't released anyone," says Jim. "I expect your girlfriend and her mother are down at that building down there, at a vigil, like."

Nikos says, "I guess."

There's no further news, so Nikos and his parents watch some television for another hour or so. Since his sisters have gone off to college it has been only Nikos and his folks in the house, and it has not been as lonely as Nikos expected it to be. They watch shows like *Happy Days*, *Good Times*, *Police Woman*, and *Kojak* (his father's favorite) together, and have some pretty good conversations right here in this kitchen, with the yellow curtains in the windows that his mother made herself. There are the food smells and the lingering warmth from the stove. It's the best room in the house.

In bed that night, Nikos thinks about the day to come. He's called Ray and told him that he's in. It's probably a stupid thing to do, to go into some older dude's apartment and take back a bunch of records for some girl who works up at the Arby's in Wheaton, a girl Nikos doesn't even know. He tells himself it's something like a mission, like back in those King Arthur days, knight-in-shining-armor shit. Like Ray said, an adventure.

Nikos gets up before first period and reads the *Washington Post*, section by section. He has been doing this since he was in elementary school, because this is what he has seen his parents do and he enjoys it. He is not a book reader but reading the newspaper on a daily basis is what has taught him how to organize his thoughts on paper in a logical and fluid manner. Meaning, it has taught him how to write. He doesn't know this now but this one habit of his will later determine the course of his life.

In the newspaper, the coverage of the Hanafi Siege (as it is now being called) is extensive. As of the morning, the intruders still control the three buildings and multiple hostages. There has been no progress or resolution.

In first-period gym, Coach lets the boys play basketball out in the parking lot without supervision. Nikos is guarded by Blake Christianson, a jock who, unbeknownst to Blake Christianson, has reached his peak. He's a bully and he likes to slight Nikos because he can. Nikos dribbles, drives by Christianson on the left, makes an underhand layup, checks the ball out, then blows by Christianson again with the same successful move. "Faggot," says Christianson to Nikos.

Nikos doesn't think he can take Christianson in a fight, but he knows he can best him on the court, so he takes the ball at the top of the key and executes the same move a third time, leaving Christianson red-faced and furious. "Game," says one of the other players, a Black kid named Rod who nods at Nikos, as if to say *You played that right.* Since junior year, Nikos's best friend, Tony, has been having sex with Christianson's longtime girlfriend, who has told Tony that Christianson is a premature ejaculator who can't "get it in." It's odd what high schoolers know about each other and keep secret. It is widespread knowledge that two teachers at their school are having affairs with students, and apparently not one kid has reported it—not even to their parents.

After fourth period, when his school day is done, Nikos drives down Georgia Avenue and meets Ed and Ray outside the shop. They get into his Belvedere, Ed in the front seat, Ray on the rear bench. Ed's casual, in a windbreaker and sneakers. Ray's wearing his cheap polyester work shirt, slacks, and hard shoes because he doesn't own any other kind of clothing.

"Let's go get Brad," says Ray.

They head on over to Hyattsville in Prince George's County, Maryland. Nikos doesn't have much occasion to be in that area, except when he goes to the Queens Chapel Drive-In, where he and Tony get their exploitation, blaxploitation, and chop-socky education in one place. Kids in Montgomery County tend to avoid PG, because the cops there have a reputation for being hostile and sometimes brutal to teenagers who are pulled over with open beers, or with pot in their glove boxes.

Bradford lives in a run-down apartment complex off Agar Road. Ray leads Ed and Nikos to his spot and knocks on his door. Bradford answers. He seems jumpy as he greets them. Ray introduces him as Brad. To Nikos, the name conjures up images of a clean-cut fraternity guy or private-school kid, but this Brad looks like the skinny, unpredictable dude you don't want to talk to in a bar, a guy who's transitioned from juvie hall to prison and is just now breathing his first free air in twelve years. He shakes everyone's hand, gives Ed two extra seconds of eyeball before stepping aside and letting everyone into the spot.

The apartment smells of nicotine, spoiled food, and perspiration. The unpleasant body odor that is coming off of Brad is speed sweat, but Nikos doesn't know enough about those kinds of drugs to identify it. Brad's wearing clothing that was unhip in 1972.

"Have a seat," says Brad, motioning to the dark furniture in his dark living room. The curtains are of course drawn. An image on the television shows a reporter in front of the District Building but the sound is turned off. Typical of burnouts, the stereo is playing at the same time. Today it's Nazareth's *Hair of the Dog*. Stroke magazines with unretouched photographs of homely girls, the kind of rags you find behind the woodshed, lie on the cable-spool table before the couch.

Brad has rolled a joint and he promptly lights it up. He and Ray smoke it down and laugh about something. Nikos and Ed turn down the jay when it gets offered to them. Nikos wouldn't mind some but the presence of Ed dissuades him.

"So what are we doing?" says Ed, getting impatient.

"We'll head out in a minute," says Brad. He produces

a few black pills from a pocket of his jeans, breaks the capsules open, and spills white powder onto a glass paperweight. He tracks the powder out with a single-edge blade. He and Ray take turns snorting it. Ray pinches his nostrils afterward and winces.

"Whew," says Ray.

"Is that coke?" says Nikos.

Nikos knows what coke is but he's not yet seen it. It hasn't really hit his high school or his peers yet. It's too expensive, for one. Some of the girls at his school who are dating older guys are doing it, but that's about it. Cocaine is for rock stars, Hollywood actors, and people who live in New York City.

"Fuck, no." says Brad. "Better. You want some?"

"No," says Nikos.

"It's go-fast," says Ray.

"Let's get outta this piece," says Ed. "Too stuffy in here."

Brad splits open more capsules of the black beauties and pours their powder into a film canister, which he pockets. He lights a cigarette, the last one from his deck, and crumples the empty package. He stands and says, "I'll be right back," and goes off into his bedroom.

"How you know this idiot?" says Ed to Ray.

"I met him at a bar," says Ray with a shrug.

"He got a job?"

"He's my dealer."

"That's his job? *Shit*."

Brad returns wearing a loose jacket. Something is

weighing down the right-hand jacket pocket. Ed's eyes clock it.

In the lot, they all get inside the Plymouth.

"Drive over to Greenbelt," says Brad.

Nikos heads in that direction. He's a little excited. He's not sorry he came today, not yet, but he's glad Ed is in the car.

They go up Route 1 past Maryland U and then east on Route 198, which is called University Boulevard where Nikos lives but here is known as Greenbelt Road. The AM radio is set to WWDC, a top-forty station, and in between "You Light Up My Life" and "Dream Weaver" the DJ gives the latest news on the Hanafi Siege, which is nothing new at all.

"Nicky has a little girlfriend," says Ray to Brad, both of them in the back seat. "Hot little number."

"Yeah?"

"Her father is one of the hostages in that Jewish building down there."

"They should drop a bomb on those ragheads," says Brad, then adds one of the redneck expressions of wisdom popular at the time: "Let God sort 'em out."

"Dumbass" says Ed, under his breath.

"Hey, pull over, Champ," says Brad. "I need cigarettes."

Nikos figures he's talking about the 7-Eleven knockoff up ahead, so he pulls into its lot. It's a place with a blue and red sign, called the Five-Ten Mart.

"I'll be right back," says Brad, who gets out of the car.

"I need cigarettes, too," says Ed, and as he steps out Nikos does the same and follows him inside. Ray stays where he sits.

The market is laid out like a 7-Eleven, but with lower lighting and more beer. There's a young guy behind the counter, Indian or Pakistani, Nikos doesn't know which. Nikos thinks the guy's got the look of someone who is too smart to be working here, as if he's on his way to somewhere better. A future engineer, something like that. In five years he'll be making more money than any of the customers in this dump. Or maybe Nikos is just stereotyping him. Could be the kid's no math or science whiz, he's just a young guy like Nikos who's into music, sports, and girls. This is his immigrant father's place and he's manning it just for today.

Brad steps up to the counter. "Marlboro Reds box," he says to the guy, whose name tag reads BASHEER.

Basheer pushes a deck of cigarettes across the counter, Brad drops a dollar there. As he rings up the sale, Ed notices Brad checking out the stacks of green in the open register.

"While you got that working," says Ed, "give me a soft-pack of Kools."

Basheer executes the sale and closes the register. Ed thanks the guy, then turns to Nikos. "You about to get anything?"

Nikos would like a roll of SweeTARTS but he's embarrassed to buy candy in front of the older men, so he says, "No."

"Take it easy, Haji," says Brad to Basheer. Basheer's eyes fade from good nature to disappointment at the slight, undeserved since he has been nothing but polite to these customers.

Out in the parking lot, Ed says to Brad, "Why you have to call him that? He didn't do a damn thing to you."

"So?" says Brad. "He's one of those sim, sim, salabim motherfuckers. I can't stand 'em. And look, if you don't like it…"

"If I don't like it, *what*?"

They've stopped walking. Brad and Ed are now in a stare-down. Brad cuts his eyes away first. His posture shrinks and he mumbles something unintelligible. He's been punked and he doesn't like it. All three of them continue on to the car.

The Springhill Lake apartments are a sprawling, multi-acre complex of garden-style units housing college students, families, young people in the early stages of their careers, and folks who work at the nearby Goddard Space Flight Center.

Still in the car, in the parking lot, Brad and Ray do bumps of speed off the crook of Brad's hand. Bullets of sweat have appeared on Brad's forehead and his eyes are bright. Nikos looks at him in the rearview and thinks of his parents. He has a secret life like all kids but whatever he does on the street, he doesn't like to bring it home. This is one of those times he's glad they're not around. He doesn't want to disappoint his mom and dad.

"All right," says Brad. "This guy, this *fucker*, his name

is Bob, he works for the government or sumshit so I know he's not home. I have a key to his place, my girl gave it to me, so we don't have to do anything but go inside his crib, take her records back, and bolt."

No one says anything, but it's a safe bet that Nikos, Ed, and Ray (yes, even Ray) are thinking the same thing: *Why would a girl in high school get involved with a greasy low-life like Brad?* The answer comes to them all fairly quickly: free weed and drugs.

They get out of the Plymouth and furtively walk toward the target unit. It's up on the second floor. On the landing, Brad knocks on the door. No one answers. He knocks again and gets the same result. Brad produces a key, fits it into the lock, and miraculously it turns. They enter.

The apartment is dark, neat and orderly, with mannish box-style furniture, chairs and sofas with oak arms and plaid upholstery. There's a nice Sansui stereo system along one wall and on the carpet before it sit records in three steel milk crates.

"There they are," says Brad.

From the front-facing albums—Boston's debut, *Left-overture* by Kansas, and the ubiquitous Eagles record, *Their Greatest Hits*—Nikos sees nothing he would want for his collection.

"Which ones are hers?" says Ray.

"We'll take them all," says Brad. "She deserves to get something extra out of this."

Brad's unable to stand still. He laughs suddenly and,

in an amphetaminic, herky-jerky motion, sweeps a full ashtray off the living-room table. It spills onto the white shag carpet, staining it gray.

"Hey," says Ed. "There's no call for that."

Brad ignores him and goes to a bar cart, pours himself three fingers from a bottle of Jack Daniels. He shotguns the mash and uses the back of his hand to wipe his mouth.

"Anybody?" says Brad. "It's on Bob."

"I'll take a pop," says Ray. Now he and Brad are standing by the bar cart. Brad is pouring out a shot for Ray and another for himself as if they live here.

Nikos can feel his blood surge. There's something red-hot about being here like this. Nikos and Tony, drunk one night on rum and beer, entered a neighborhood house for kicks and stood in the basement until they heard someone stirring upstairs. It feels like that now. They haven't broken into this apartment, exactly, but that's a technicality. If caught they'd be charged with all kinds of crimes. Nikos is scared, but he's exhilarated, too.

"Hey, Nicky," says Ed. "Why don't you go out and start the car? Pop the trunk, too. We'll be out straight-away. Isn't that *right*, Ray?"

"Sure, yeah, go ahead, Nicky," says Ray, reading Ed's tone.

Nikos leaves the place and quick-steps to his Belve-dere. He unlocks the trunk and leaves the lid ajar, then gets under the wheel. He turns the ignition and waits. Inside the apartment he felt safe but out here alone fear starts to overtake him, along with regret.

"Stupid," he says, in a rare moment of self-reflection.

Soon Ray, Ed, and Brad come out, each of them carrying a crate of records in their arms. There are people walking to and from their vehicles but the thieves are paid no mind. The men place the crates in the trunk of the Plymouth. The car drops slightly from the weight. They get into the Belvedere.

"Success, motherfuckers," says Brad. To Nikos he says, "Drive."

Nikos feels a rush of relief as they pull out of the lot and head west on Greenbelt Road. That feeling subsides as they near the Five-Ten Mart they visited earlier and Brad says, "Stop in there, I wanna get some beer."

"You can get beer near your crib," says Ed.

"I want a beer now," says Brad. "Pull over."

Nikos does it. He's trying to avoid conflict in the car. He pulls into a space facing the road.

"I'll be right back," says Brad.

In one fluid motion, Ed turns in his seat, grabs Brad by the lapels of his shirt, and pulls him forward violently, so that he is right up in Brad's face.

"You ain't going *no* goddamn where," says Ed.

"Whoa," says Brad, his hands immediately rising. "*Relax*, man."

"Don't *man* me, boy. I know you're about to rob that kid in there. You got a heater in the right pocket of your jacket, Brad, and your jacked-up, junkie ass is fixin to use it."

"Look, I was just...It's easy money. The cops are all

focused on those fucking Arabs downtown. There's no law here today."

Nikos's hands are bloodless, tight on the steering wheel. For a long beat, it's silent in the car. A few months earlier, at a house party, a kid pulled a steak knife on Nikos in the kitchen, for no other reason than he was cooked on alcohol. The people in the kitchen said nothing, and time slowed down, until an older guy talked the kid down and took the knife. It feels like that now.

"Ray," says Ed, "reach into your boy's pocket and take his gun."

Ray does it. He hands it over the seat to Ed, who releases Brad. It's a .38 with a brown checkered grip. Nikos recognizes it because his father owns one like it. Ed pockets the gun.

Brad lowers his hands. "*You.*"

"Shut the fuck up," says Ed, tiredly. To Nikos he says, "Take this asshole back to his place and drop him off."

No one speaks on the ride into Hyattsville. In Brad's parking lot, strewn with trash and grocery carts, everyone gets out as Nikos opens the trunk. Ed tells Brad to unload the crates of records himself. Brad does it grudgingly, and then, the crates set on the asphalt of the lot, says, "Isn't anyone gonna help me get these inside?"

Ed breaks the cylinder on Brad's revolver, shakes the live rounds out of the wheel, pockets the bullets, and tosses the empty gun to Brad.

"Let's go," says Ed. He and Nikos climb into the

Plymouth. Ray doesn't look at Brad as he gets into the
back seat.

No one speaks as Nikos drives over to Langley Park,
where Ray lives in a one-bedroom apartment off New
Hampshire Avenue. They drop Ray in front of his building.

"I'll see you guys tomorrow," says Ray, as if nothing
has happened.

Nikos and Ed watch him go into his place, passing
Latino kids playing on the front lawn.

"Drop me at my car," says Ed.

Ed drives a clean, '74 Grand Prix with opera windows.
It's parked on Peabody Street, not far from the store. As
Nikos pulls up behind it, Ed points to the key dangling in
the ignition and says, "Kill it."

It's late in the afternoon, moving to evening. Shadows
have begun to lengthen on the street.

"I hope you learned something today," says Ed.

Nikos just nods. He's still processing what happened
back in the parking lot of the market.

"You shouldn't be hanging around with people like
Ray Baumann outside of work. *Or* his low friends. You
shouldn't have been there today at all."

"I hear you," says Nikos. He hears him *now*.

Nikos has figured out that Ed came along today to
look after him. It's strange because Ed in the past has not
given him much more than the time of day.

There are many things Nikos would like to ask him.
*How did he know Brad was about to rob the market? How did
he know Brad had a gun?* But he doesn't ask those questions

because he realizes that he's out of his league. Ed is experienced, for real. A guy who lived through Jim Crow D.C. in his childhood. A guy who fought and was injured in an actual war. Nikos is still a kid who's grown up in the suburbs. He doesn't know shit from apple butter.

Instead, Nikos asks him what is foremost in his mind. "Are we gonna get in trouble for what we did?"

"I expect not," says Ed. "This Bob character will probably figure out that it was his ex-girlfriend who set the whole thing up, on account of we used the key that he gave her. But why would he report it? He lost a few records, is all. If he gets the police involved, he's got to go into court eventually and talk about how he, a grown-ass man with a government job, was in a relationship with a high-school girl. I think he'll just change the locks on his crib and write off the loss."

"I hope so," says Nikos.

"So what did you learn today?" says Ed.

"Not to do stupid stuff?"

"It's more than that. You think Ray Baumann is cool, with his rap and his hustle, right? You think he's street, and that's what you aspire to."

"Not really..."

"Sure you do. Wasn't too long ago I was young. I looked up to dudes like him, too, in the pool halls and in the neighborhood. But I was wrong, and so are you. Look, Ray *likes* you, man, but only because you hero-worship his ass. You about the last one who doesn't see him for what he is. Take my word for it, he's gonna do you dirt. Shoot, he almost *did* mess you over today. You could have been party to an armed robbery."

"I didn't know."

"Look, young man, you got a lot of things in your favor. You don't know it, but you're smarter than most. You come from a stable home. You got a mother and father who care about you...That's a big deal, more than you know. Don't get caught up in all this bullshit. Think about who you're hanging with, hear?"

"Yes."

"And one more thing. That girlfriend of yours?"

"Mindy?"

"You need to treat that young lady with respect. I heard you talking to Ray about her one day, how you got *with* her in the back seat of your car."

Nikos blushes and squirms in his seat.

"Yeah, that's right," said Ed. "Bragging on what you did. Why you tellin on her to Ray like that?"

"I shouldn't. You're right."

"After you make time with her, you ever send that girl flowers? Give her a card, anything like that?"

"I never have. No."

"Think about it." Ed exhales slowly. "Okay, then. I've given you enough advice for one day. Let me get on home. My wife is expecting me for supper."

"Thanks, Ed."

"Be safe."

Nikos watches Ed walk to his Pontiac in the gathering dusk.

———————

Nikos has dinner with his parents that evening. He's quiet and evasive. When they ask him what he's done all day after school he says he "played basketball down at the courts."

It's spaghetti night. Every Thursday his mother serves her sauce, a delicious, slow-cooked concoction whose secret weapon is a whole pork chop that falls apart in the pot after several hours and subtly flavors the mix. His father is wearing his white work shirt with the sleeves rolled to the elbows. He's drinking a Budweiser from an amber glass. Jim doesn't like beer particularly, but it's his doctor's advice to drink one every night to ward off another bout of kidney stones, which he has suffered from in the past.

The thirteen-inch black-and-white shows an image of a reporter outside the District Building. The siege has not ended but there appears to be some progress. Officials have not acceded to any of Hamaas Khaalis's demands (they won't, due to the murder of WHUR reporter Maurice Williams), but the ambassadors of Pakistan, Iran, and Egypt have been persuaded to come to Khaalis and try to convince him to release the hostages. Right now they are in the building, reading Khaalis relevant passages from the Koran.

"Smart," says Jim Tzirimis. "They brought his own kind in there to talk him down. They're reading to him from that book they got."

"It's their Bible," says Nikos.

"That's the book where they say it's okay to chop someone's head off?"

"Our Bible's got plenty of violent stuff in it, too."

"What are you, a theologian, now?"

"Yeah, Dad. I'm gonna enter the seminary after I graduate."

"You'd have to stop messing around with girls," says his father, and then with a gleam in his eye, he says, "and playing with your pecker."

"*Dimitri*," says Elaine. She calls him that only when she's admonishing him for something, or when she's being affectionate, which oftentimes is the same thing.

"Just saying," says Jim. "There's something in the Bible about spilling your seed. It says that God's against it."

"I'm sure that never stopped you," says Elaine, and then she chuckles nervously. There's a look between husband and wife that makes Nikos feel like he shouldn't be there.

After an uncomfortable silence, Nikos says, "I think I'm going to go down to the B'nai B'rith building tonight. I haven't been able to get hold of Mindy. I just want to, like, be there for her."

"I don't know if that's a good idea," says Elaine. "You might be out late, and you have school in the morning."

His mother isn't a big fan of Mindy. It might be because she's Jewish, but then she probably wouldn't like any girl he was with.

"All he does at school is play basketball," says Jim. "He can go if he wants to."

That settles it.

"How was the sauce?" says his mother to Nikos.

"Delicious, Ma."

After Elaine clears the plates, they sit in the kitchen together and watch an episode of *Barney Miller* and, after that, *The Streets of San Francisco*.

Nikos is thankful for dodging a bullet earlier in the day. Now he's here, and he's safe. Many of his friends can't wait to get out of high school and leave their homes and their parents behind. Sometimes Nikos will be in a car with others and they'll pick up another random boy at his house. When the boy gets into the car, he says, viciously, "I hate my mom," or, "Fuck my dad." Nikos is always a little astonished at that, because he never even thinks those words in his head. He feels sorry for kids who feel that way. He's not in any hurry for his life to change, even though he knows it soon will.

Late that night Nikos peeks into his parents' bedroom and tells them again that he's headed out.

"Be careful, honey," says Elaine. His father, who gets up at 4:30 every day to meet the bread man and the iceman at his diner (which in their home is called the *magazi*), is already out and snoring.

Nikos drives downtown, parks a few blocks north of 16th and Rhode Island Avenue. The police, newspaper, and television-news presence is heavy, along with spectators. He gets as close as he can to the B'nai B'rith building.

After some searching, he sees Mindy and her mother, Evie Goldman, toward the front of the crowd, along with others who are waiting to hear about their loved ones.

Nikos doesn't try to make his way over to them. It would be inappropriate for him to intrude upon their circle tonight. Plus, Mindy's mother and father don't care for him. They've pushed her to socialize with guys at the JCC, just as Nikos's parents have encouraged him to date girls from his church. It's not that her folks dislike non-Jews, not that he's aware of, anyway. It's that they know he's having sex with their daughter. He's not going to be their son-in-law. They're just kids. Mindy has no future with him. It's as simple as that.

At around two in the morning the crowd begins to stir and some people cheer and hug. After thirty-seven hours, the hostages are being released. As they slowly come out of the building, they are reunited with their loved ones. Nikos sees Mr. Goldman join his wife and daughter in a tight embrace. Evie Goldman is crying. Nikos makes no move to join them. Instead he waits, and finally catches Mindy's eye. She gives him a smile but stays with her parents.

Nikos walks to his Belvedere. That's all he wanted to do, to let Mindy know that he was thinking of her. Ed's voice has been talking to him in his head.

Ed was right about Ray, but Nikos isn't smart enough yet to take Ed's immediate advice.

A few weeks after the Hanafi Siege, Ray asks Nikos if he'd like to get Mindy and "double date" with Ray and his latest girlfriend, a woman named Louise. They're invited out to Louise's town house in Olney, a far suburb of D.C.

Nikos thinks it's just going to be a night of getting high and listening to some records, and it is, at first. The four of them are all smoked up, *Ask Rufus* is playing on the stereo, and that has put them in a mood. Louise, a too-thin woman in her mid-thirties, heavily made up with thick eyeliner, asks Nikos to "give her hand for a minute" in the kitchen, she's going to put out some cheese and crackers.

He politely follows her to a kitchen that is well off the living room. She doesn't make a move to get any food, but instead comes close to him and asks him if it's "warm in here." He kind of shrugs and then she says, "I'm hot, Nicky. Are you hot?" She raises the nipples of her breasts through her shirt, which she twists with her fingers. Nikos has not been expecting this, to say the least. Maybe he's been naïve and has not read any of the signs. Though she's a youngish woman, she's an old woman to him, eighteen years his senior. It's as if one of his mother's friends is coming on to him. He's not turned on, he's confused. He backs up and says, lamely, "I'm not hot, I'm fine."

Louise looks a little disappointed, but not at all ashamed, and she and Nikos go back out to the living room. Ray has moved over to the couch beside Mindy, who gives Nikos a meaningful stare. They stay a little longer, until Nikos says something about "a long day," and he and Mindy split.

Out in the car, Nikos tells Mindy that Louise came on to him in the kitchen.

Mindy says, "Ray hit on me, too."

"They planned it," says Nikos.

"He's gross," says Mindy.

The next day, at work, Ray doesn't even mention what happened the night before. Nikos realizes that in Ray's mind he has done nothing wrong.

Three months later, Nikos has graduated from high school, left his job at Payless Appliance and Mattresses, and gotten a summer job at an auto-parts store, where he drives a quarter-ton, white Ford Courier and does route delivery to area gas stations. The AM radio in the truck plays "Smoke from a Distant Fire," "Cold as Ice," and "Fly Like an Eagle" in heavy rotation. Mindy and Nikos's best friend, Tony, leave town for out-of-state colleges.

Nikos has enrolled at the University of Maryland, College Park, because it's cheap and close to home. He doesn't really know why he's going to college but it's expected of him and he doesn't want to let his parents down. He's lonely on campus; he doesn't know anyone, and he's not in a fraternity or a dorm. He takes a part-time job at the Luskins-Dalmo in Landover Mall, selling electronics and appliances, which is fun for him, more fun than classes. He tells his father, "Maybe I'll forget college, just sell TVs and stereos for a living, I can make twenty-five grand a year," and his father says, "Bullshit, you're going to get a degree," and that's the end of the discussion.

In his second semester he takes a journalism class and things begin to change. Nikos gets on the staff of the highly regarded daily student newspaper, and he finds his tribe. He's lost touch with Mindy long ago. They stopped writing each other letters when she found a boyfriend in her first semester at the University of Miami. For his part, Nikos plays the field.

One night, he's been in the bars in Georgetown, drinking downtown for hours with a young woman named Sharon, and they're driving up 16th Street. They've already made out and had their hands on each other and neither of them can wait. Nikos makes a left off 16th and pulls his car to the curb on Tuckerman Street and kills the engine. Vaguely, he's aware that he's two short blocks from the Hanafi House on Van Buren, but he's not spooked by it anymore. He's ripped on alcohol and cocaine, and he wants what he wants, and so does Sharon. They walk up Tuckerman and cut north into an alley that connects to Underwood Street and then they walk west to Underwood's dead end and step onto the Rock Creek Park Golf Course. They're on a green. He doesn't know what hole it is but it's manicured and pristine, and at night it's deserted, and the two of them make it on the damp grass. He's done this before with other girls, right here. It's one of his secret spots in D.C.

He hasn't grown much with regard to women. He's careless with them, and in his mind he and Sharon are just having a good time. He has something of an awakening when a year later he's DUI'd with a woman in his car, a woman who is not Sharon but like her, someone he might have killed while driving drunk, someone he has treated thoughtlessly. He cuts down on alcohol, gives up drugs, and straightens his shit out.

After college he takes a job at the *Austin American-Statesman* (where he meets his future wife, Amelia, a features writer), then the *Albuquerque Journal*, where deep in his thirties he is an award finalist (not the Pulitzer) for a series of articles he has written on police corruption. The nomination brings him to the attention of editors at the *Washington Post*, who offer him a job on the crime beat in his hometown. He flourishes at the *Post* and spends the rest of his career there.

Nikos is sixty-three. He can hardly believe it. His parents have passed. He is a grandfather. He has lived through the experience of distrusting and secretly disliking the boys who dated his daughters (now both married) in high school, knowing their intentions because he was just like them. He and Amelia are in the process of figuring out "what to do" when they retire. That day is coming soon.

But for now he writes. He's working on a story about a mass shooting in April 1975, when a lone white gunman shot seven Black people, killing two, in Wheaton, Maryland. It has haunted Nikos since he was fifteen years old, when he watched the news of the shooting in real time with his parents, on the small television set in the kitchen of their home. The shooting happened just a mile from his house. But now, when he brings it up in conversation with locals, very few remember it. They seem to think that the racial shootings in places like Charleston are something new.

Nikos thinks it's important to get the Wheaton shooting down on record. If he doesn't write it, it will be as if it never happened.

He's written about the Murder House and the Hanafi Siege as well. It has brought back that time to him and how he felt. It has helped him own up to who he was.

He's had no contact with Mindy for over forty years. He sees from her Facebook page that she has been in a longtime marriage and that she, too, has grandchildren. He thinks about the times in high school when they were in the back seat of his Plymouth Belvedere, and he knew she didn't really want to, but she let him have her because it was easier than arguing about it. Or, in that same back seat, when she'd say she had to get home, that her parents had given her a curfew, and he'd say, "C'mon, you can be half an hour late, it's okay," and then he'd have sex with her. He knows now that she was saying no. But he was too selfish to listen.

After he left Payless Appliances and Mattresses, Nikos never spoke to Ray or Ed again. He hasn't thought of Ray much, or how he looked up to him. That, too, feels like it was another life. Nikos saw an obituary for Ed ten years earlier. He regrets losing touch with him. He hopes that Ed saw Nikos's byline in the *Post*, recognized his name, and felt that he had made some kind of difference in the young man's growth.

Nikos doesn't live too far from his childhood neighborhood. He's a cyclist, in decent shape for a guy in his sixties. He rides his bike over there occasionally, and stops in front of his parents' house. He doesn't know anyone on the street anymore. They've all moved or have passed.

The house has been painted, and a new portico has been built above the stoop, but the birch and dogwood trees, which his mother loved, still stand in the front yard. Nikos can see his bedroom, and the larger bedroom where his sisters slept, up on the second floor. The kitchen is in the back of the house. He can't see it from the street. He can imagine it, though, and he does, clearly. The round Formica-top table, the thirteen-inch black-and-white television on the rolling stand, the yellow curtains his mother sewed herself. He can smell her spaghetti sauce simmering on the stove.

ACKNOWLEDGMENTS

Many thanks to Josh Kendall of Mulholland Books for his thoughtful editing on this collection, and to copyeditors Betsy Uhrig and Allan Fallow for bringing it over the finish line. Thanks to Sabrina Callahan and her publicity team at Little, Brown for their hard work, and to Michael Pietsch for his guidance. I'm indebted to Sloan Harris and Kevin Crotty at CAA and Ron West at Thruline Entertainment for their continued efforts on my behalf. Thanks to Emad Akhtar at Orion Books in the UK and Robert Pepin at Editions Calmann-Levy in France. A grateful nod to the Historical Society of Washington, D.C., for their assistance and kindness.

ABOUT THE AUTHOR

GEORGE PELECANOS is the bestselling author of twenty-two
novels and story collections set in and around Washington, D.C. He is also an independent-film producer, and
a producer and Emmy-nominated writer on the HBO
series *The Wire*, *Treme*, *The Deuce*, and *We Own This City*.
He lives in Maryland.